Snap Justice

By

Ken Olive

Also by Ken Olive:

Goldie's Garden

Special Corps

Publisher: Ken Olive Publishing

ISBN-13: 978-0-615-41654-0
ISBN-10: 0-615-41654-3

First Edition: November 2010

10 9 8 7 6 5 4 3 2 1

One

Just as the dream dissolved, Paige Anders tried to remember the nightmare of the previous evening. It was a mix of confusion, followed by blackout. She had a strange taste in her mouth and had been convulsing with the dry heaves.

Paige was blindfolded. She still had her overcoat on, which was good because there was a rare "freeze warning" for tonight. It wasn't typically this cold in San Antonio during January.

Her hands and feet were somehow secured. She could smell the dank, earthy floor of what could only be an old basement. But a basement where? She lived in Olmos Park, a distinctive part of San Antonio. Her condo didn't have a basement. Someone had brought her here. Why?

Almost in answer to her unspoken question, Paige heard muffled footsteps coming toward her. It sounded as if someone were walking on paper. It was a rustling sound.

"Is someone there?" she asked. "What do you want? I've got money, you can have it." There was no response forthcoming. Nothing verbal, anyway. The feeling of a foreign presence grew stronger. Suddenly, Paige felt two cold objects on the back of her neck. She strained to escape the icy, metal feeling. She tried to rise, but was unable to do so. Then the lights went out, even behind the blindfold.

They'd been warned, thought the "Taker". They'd been warned twice. Now they would have to take notice and realize the consequences of their inactions. There had been no idle threats, only promises of things to come when a job was left undone. This was not enjoyment, it was a responsibility.

Two

Toni (Antonia) Ramos assembled her squad on the third floor for their usual 9 am meeting at police headquarters on Nueva St. in the center of San Antonio. It was at this daily meeting that she received progress reports for ongoing investigations, reviewed recent events, and passed out new assignments.

However, this was Monday, and as was par for all Mondays, police reports contained more drunken shootings, fist fights, stabbings, and lots of various weekend violence. Most of this increase in crime was due to the average citizenry, starting off with the best of intentions. The community had plenty of weddings, birthdays, funerals, etc. planned for every weekend. It was at these "family" events that someone always drank just a little bit too much, or tried to make out with the wrong person's significant other, or just said something which was taken as being disrespectful.

These family gatherings held the opportunity for brawls, begun by the dominate males attending all these get-togethers. Hopefully, most would only result in a broken hand or arm, and a call to SAPD. The police cruiser would roll into a group of people huddled in a picnic area, all pointing at everyone else as being the instigator. In the end, no one saw anything...amazing? Uncle Freddie just tripped, cousin Bobby, was showing off and hurt himself...no problem officer, thanks for coming out, etc., etc.

About once a weekend, one of these encounters would escalate to knives or handguns, with the occasional multiple injuries or even death, involved. This was the saddest part of police work. Family against family, lives shattered, futures destroyed. For what, Toni asked, Por que?

From the reports Toni saw in front of her, it seemed to be more of the same. Every morning report is a bitch, Toni thought to herself, but Mondays are going to be the death of me.

She wasn't the first female squad leader, nor the first Hispanic. Thank God, others had paved the way for her. But, she thought, she was the best, at least so far. Toni's jet black hair offset a fair complexion, and she was just as shapely and attractive as when she graduated UTSA, eight years ago. She ran marathons for a while, before an ACL strain put a halt to her running. Her squad of twelve investigators had a reputation as being among the best in the department. They had a solid case clearance record, and seldom lost in the courtroom because they hadn't been professional.

Her squad reported to the homicide Lieutenant, Don Daniels, then to Captain Torres of the major crimes section, and Captain Bernardo, of SAPD Investigations. Bernardo was the last working cop on the depth chart. In this city of 1.5 million people, 60% who were of Hispanic background, he wielded a heavy, but even, hand. He reported to Chief Perez, a politician, if there ever was one. Law enforcement in a city this large, and this diverse, only two hours from the Mexican border, was possibly the biggest challenge in the country. Drugs and gangs here, were just as pervasive as in L.A. or Houston.

Toni rose to begin her duty call when a clerk cracked open the duty room door and spied her. "Detective Ramos," she said, "they want you upstairs, on 7". Toni responded, "Thirty minutes, I'm just beginning my meeting."

"Sorry," the clerk said, "Captain Bernardo said now!" Toni knew what a command performance was, it used to be ordered by HRM, to those fortunate enough to grovel at the feet of the English Monarch. This was no less intimidating. Toni gathered her operational material and passed it to sergeant Olivia, to continue, no, actually to hold the entire squad meeting. Usually, meetings on the 7th floor were not jovial or back-slapping. Something was up. And it sounded big.

Toni grabbed a legal pad, a habit of hers which had served her well in the past, and took the elevator up to 7. As she stepped off the elevator, she couldn't help but be aware of the police brass and myriad political figures milling around the lobby. This was HQ for the SAPD Special Investigations Office. Obviously, the Chief was already there, down from his Ivory Tower on the 9th floor.

Toni was seated in the entry foyer for 15 minutes until the captain's assistant opened the inner door, saw her, and waved her into the inner sanctum.

She entered and saw the law enforcement and political heavyweights arrayed before her around a large conference table. From the deputy mayor, two city councilmen, to the Police Chief, and all other attendees, everyone's eyes were now focused on her.

She instinctively questioned if she or someone in her squad had done something wrong. Had they given a speeding ticket to the governor, insulted the mayor. No, she couldn't think of anything. OK, so far, so good.

Captain Bernardo stood up, "Have a seat," he boomed, gesturing to a chair halfway down the table. Toni stumbled to it, somehow, sat, and placed her legal pad and pen in front of her. She turned to face Chief Perez. He commented, glancing at the pad, "Very thorough, that's why you're here. You know most of the people in the room. Those that you don't, you'll learn very quickly, he said." The chief added, "Anything said in this room today will be strictly confidential. Is that understood?" Toni replied, "Yes, Chief Perez, absolutely." She knew that the SAPD, mayor's office, and the other departments represented here today, were riddled with leaks. Hell, the streets probably had the outline of the meeting, already.

Captain Bernardo began, "We've had two murders of note in our city in the past month. When I say of note, we've averaged 3 to 4 killings a week for the past 2 years. A great deal of it gang or drug related, or both. But, we've had two identical, deliberate murders which bear more scrutiny."

Toni saw the specter of politics rear it's ugly head. Ten gangbangers shot, no big deal. One clean (non-criminal) citizen was a disaster. Apparently, we had two. And this was about tossing the hot potato. The captain let his opening statement sink in, and continued, "Two young career females, one Anglo, and one Hispanic, have been killed. We need to find out who did it and arrest him. Simple enough?"

And, you need a woman to lead the investigation, Toni thought, but dared not say. Actually, it sounded to her like it could possibly be a plum assignment. She asked Captain Bernardo, "What makes you sure they're connected?"

He explained, "M.O., cause of death, lots of similar crime scene information, and the opinions of several professionals who you will hear from today. We don't put the tag 'serial killer' on any event without being absolutely certain. You listen to the experts here, and make up your own mind. If you disagree, afterward, we can talk." Right, Toni thought. Someone's mind is made up, and he's my boss's, boss's, boss. And I'm going to argue?

Without further elaboration, The Captain turned to one of the other people at the table and asked, "Doctor Alexander, your findings, please."

Doctor Samuel Alexander, was the head medical examiner for Bexar county, for which San Antonio was the county seat. He rose from his chair with two thick manila envelopes. He was in his late thirties, a graduate of the University of Texas Medical school.

He had held this position for over 4 years, and had established an excellent record for the department. He was about six feet tall, average build, brownish hair, attractive, and married. Toni always did her homework. Well, there were other reasons she had looked up his resume.

Doctor Alexander read from the first file, "Angela Mendez, age twenty six, CPA with a local accounting firm, died somewhere between 2 and 4 am, December 12th. Her body was discovered in a mining quarry on the east side of San Antonio. She had been killed elsewhere and dumped there, we're sure of that."

He continued, "Tox screens uncovered alcohol at .09%, slightly above the legal driving limit of .07%, but was not a factor in her death. We did uncover a high level of Rohypnol, also called 'roofies' the date-rape drug. It was sufficient to incapacitate her, but again, was not the cause of death."

Toni raised her hand, as if in a classroom, "Was she sexually assaulted?" To which the doctor responded, "There was no evidence of sexual assault anywhere on the body nor was there any signs of ritual masturbation. This was a cold blooded murder, not the work of an attempted rapist," the doctor concluded.

"Please continue, doctor," the Captain asked. Alexander continued his report, "Cause of death was separation of the spinal column between C-3 and C-4, resulting in total body shutdown and instantaneous death."

Again, her hand rose, "Could this have been a result of a fall or accident? Maybe she fell down a set of stairs at a party and a panicked boyfriend dumped her body somewhere so his life wouldn't come under scrutiny. Is that possible?"

"Let me finish, first, then I'll answer you," he said. Toni wasn't trying to antagonize the doctor, she just offered some alternatives. Toni was being Toni, which meant she first wanted to eliminate all doubt. You could never take things at face value. If you did, you were usually wrong, she had learned that, the hard way.

Dr. Alexander picked up the second file. "Two nights ago, January 11th, between 2 and 3 am, I can be more precise on time of death, as the ambient temperature was far cooler," he added, "Paige Anders, age 28, an associate at a San Antonio law firm was found dead in a ditch off Huebner Road, in the west side of the city." He continued, "Again, she had most certainly been killed somewhere else, and the body was moved to the site of the discovery."

"Now, to answer your question, Detective, No," the doctor replied. "Both the spines were surgically severed. Some sort of scissor-like commercial cutter, like a tin cutter or sharpened pliers was used."

The doctor added, "Marks on the bones of the victims indicate that the same weapon was used on each, however we will have to conduct research utilizing greater magnification for that to hold up in court. I am, however, 99% confident we have an exact match. Two victims, exact M.O., both wrongful deaths, equals one serial killer, as far as I'm concerned." Toni was becoming a believer. Obviously, this was the reason for this power meeting, today. It had been hastily organized, and she thought that several people, herself included, had been notified at the last possible moment in order to preserve as much secrecy as possible.

The doctor concluded, "You swap the names on these files, and everything is exactly the same. Tox screens, time of death, cause of death, a carbon copy."

Oh boy, Toni thought, wait till the press gets into this one, and they will, probably before the meeting ends. The pressure will be enormous. And I thought this might be a great assignment. Someone in this room is going down, if this case isn't solved quickly. She thought she knew who that "someone" would be, and she didn't like the answer.

The doctor sat, and the Captain looked at a man Toni was much more familiar with, "Lieutenant Daniels, you have both crime scene reports?" Captain Bernardo asked rhetorically. "Yes sir, I have them," answered the lieutenant.

He began, "Again, for brevity's sake, let me first say that other than the location of the bodies, the crime scene reports are identical." He read from his prepared notes, "The hands and feet of both victims were bound with plastic straps, available at all the hardware or discount stores in town. We found no body fluids, no hair, no prints, full or partial, nothing under the fingernails, and no sign of defensive wounds other than ligature marks from the straps".

"All bruising of the bodies was characterized as post-mortem by Dr. Alexander, probably a result of being dumped from a vehicle."

He looked at the group and added, "I'm sorry. We stayed at these sites for hours, conducted an exhaustive investigation at both scenes, and came up empty. This person is either very thorough, or very lucky. I'm hoping for lucky, because luck always runs out."

"OK," said the Captain, "lastly we have a couple of clues from the I.T. (Internet Technology) department." An attractive woman in her mid to late thirties, stood up and introduced herself as Adrian Keller, assistant head of Internet Technology.

"We get hundreds of e-mails daily, complaining about barking dogs, girls trying to get their 'ex' in trouble, etc. We can't follow up on the most of these, but we do run the messages through a program specially designed for Homeland Security, looking for key words such as shipment, crack, meth, and so forth."

"The day after the December murder we flagged an e-mail message which contained the words murder and CPA in it. This was before the newspaper or TV knew that any killing had occurred. Screen please," she asked.

To: SAPD & DA's Office

You're Letting the Gangs run this town.

Do your jobs or I will.

You'll have more than the Murder of a CPA to deal with

When I go Public...The Taker

Holy Shit, Toni thought. Those words "go public", put a chill up the spine of every department represented in the room. The press would have the town whipped up in a frenzy. Now the thoughts and purpose behind this meeting were becoming more clear to her.

"Get out in front of it," was the old saying. Toni knew that she could be stepping in front of a freight train.

The woman continued, "After this first message, we added the words 'The Taker' to the key word filter. Yesterday, we received a message from whom we believe to be the same source. Next slide, please." It read:

To: SAPD and DA's Office

Now we're up to lawyers...do you believe me?

In 30 days the Gangs have caused 16 Deaths, just counting

those that we know of.

Do Something...The Taker

cc: The San Antonio Express News

The I.T. employee added, "Of course, both of the e-mails came in through an untraceable 'hotmail' account, so there's no way we could ever identify the owner. If it's of any political comfort, I'm sure the newspaper doesn't have access to sophisticated, e-mail filtering software like we do, but the intent to go public is there, and eventually, the media will find out."

"Young lady," Chief Perez bellowed, "this isn't about politics, it's about catching a criminal."

"Of course not sir, sorry," the computer technology expert replied meekly. Toni looked at the woman's horrified face, and stood, "She's absolutely right," she said, "and we all know it. We can't be made to look ineffective."

Toni wasn't going to let an assistant I.T. person get bullied by the Police Chief, especially when she was right. "The community will find out, and we'd better be on the job, doing what we do, when they start asking their questions."

The chief ignored Toni's defense, and wrapped up, "So Detective Ramos, I don't think there's any question of a serial killer here, do you?" Toni just shook her head, "No chief, I just wanted to make sure."

"That's why we picked you," he assured her. "You're thorough, determined, and not easily swayed." Right, Toni thought, and I'm also a young, professional female, and best of all, expendable.

Chief Perez continued to speak to Toni, "As of now, you're in charge of this task force. You're going to nail this bastard to the wall for the community. You're going to make it safe to walk the streets again." Toni thought it sounded like an election speech, maybe he was practicing. There had been no shortage of rumors flying about a mayoral bid in Perez' future.

Chief Perez added, "I want you to have at least 4 other investigators on the force, help from other divisions, plus I.T., and total access to anything else you might need. Captain Bernardo and Lieutenant Daniels will probably suggest some names for you to consider for your task force, but the final decision will be yours."

Of course, she thought, he was already leaving an exit for

himself...it was her decision, she was in charge, they were there only to provide support, blah, blah, blah. He concluded, "All overtime is approved. You will have my full support, and that of the ME's and DA's offices. If you need assistance from state, in Austin, go through Captain Bernardo. He will provide approval and be the liaison, no contacts without prior approval."

"Any and all public remarks to the media are to be approved by me, and me alone, understood, Detective ?"

"Yes, chief," she said. He rose, "I want a status report on my desk by noon each day until we catch this monster," and he left the table and walked toward a door being held open for him. Back to the 9th floor, Toni thought.

Three

Toni's head was spinning. She returned to her small office on 3, and shut the door. Instinctively, she placed her legal pad in front of her. She wrote, "Who wants to be on the Titanic?"

There was a quick rap on the door, followed by her lead investigator letting himself in. Billy Cheatham was all Texas. He led the league in looks, style, girlfriends, and BS. At 6'3" 210 pounds, the ex rodeo bull rider was built as solid as a rock. But he was also a great investigator who solved cases no one thought possible. "What's got you down, 'Tone', he asked her."

"How do you feel about jumping off a cliff with me," she asked. "I'd go anywhere with you," he snickered. "I've asked a hundred times, you keep turning me down. What's different this time?"

"I mean on a case, you big, tobacco chewing dummy, being on a task force with me and some others. A special assignment from the chief. And if we don't succeed, there won't be any parachutes for this jump." She was full of analogies, today.

Billy whistled (he couldn't chew in the building), "Sounds big," he winked, "right down my alley."

"I'm serious Cheatham...as in dead serious. You get into this, there's no going back, she warned."

"Like I said, count me in," he retorted. "OK, she said, we're having a meeting at 1:00, I'll let you know where, and not a word to anyone." Billy left, still smiling, and closed the door behind him. He's in for a big surprise, Toni thought. A lot tougher than riding a rodeo bull, or anything else he'd experienced on the job. Oh well, she thought, be careful what you ask for. Billy would find out soon enough.

Three lines under the word "Titanic" on her legal pad she wrote down 1) Cheatham. Then a blank 2), 3), 4), 5), and then "others." she knew that she wanted Rosa Padilla on the team. She was experienced, and had worked "sex crimes" division in the past. She understood the mentality of predators, and their affect on society. She was also a great interrogator, the quiet, unassuming type, who learned lots more than you intended to say during an interview.

After that, Starr Jones, a young, black female might make a good addition. She was sharp, and hungry. Starr was in a different squad, but still reported to Lieutenant Daniels.

Getting the fifth member might be awkward, but necessary. Thomas Granger had a reputation of a dinosaur. Think Clint Eastwood, without as much charm. More like "Dirty Harry", with no excuses at all. Granger was sure, that Toni had received her promotion because the department had a quota to fill...women, minorities, etc.

The fact that on occasion Tom had been brought up on charges of using excessive force with suspects, had absolutely nothing to do with it, according to him. The crooks were all scum and had no rights at all, according to Tom Granger. He was not yet 45 on his birth certificate, but he retained the old cop mentality of 20 years ago.

But, she needed someone like that, on her team. The problem would be getting him to buy-into whatever strategy they developed. What would take her or Billy an hour to wheedle out of a gang-banger, Tom could get in five minutes. He didn't have to do anything. His reputation spoke for itself. When they told even the toughest gang leader, that they were going to leave him in the interrogation room, alone, with Tom, words started flowing...it was a miracle.

Lastly, Adrian Keller, the I.T. assistant was a no-brainer. She wouldn't be going out on investigations with them, but including her on the daily briefings, supplying new key words to the software filter, telling her what scenarios they were looking for, not thinking like a cop, but like a researcher. Adrian could be a key to solving the case. All from behind a desk. The world had become much smaller the past ten years.

Now, Toni just had to sell Lieutenant Don Daniels on her picks. Toni phoned the lieutenant's office, and no surprise there, got an immediate appointment to "come on over".

She outlined the her choices for the task force, and asked for any ideas from Daniels on the structure or personnel. Toni was honest, "I need all the help or ideas I can get," she admitted.

"Well, you're in a pressure cooker, now," he started. "And by association, so am I." Two things I'm asking for, in the beginning," he continued. "I'm not sure I agree with including Tom Granger, but I see your logic. It adds balance and inclusion. He also might see it as a 'feather' in his cap."

"So the first of the two things is, I'd like the three of us, you, Tom, and me, meet before you speak to any others. That way we can clear the air from the beginning. I want Tom to realize how important he is to the project, that we want his help."

He asked, "Secondly, I'd like to briefly attend your first task force meeting, only to add some weight to the job. You and I are going to be feeling that weight. I want them to know that shit rolls downhill. Do you have any problem with that? I don't want to usurp your authority, just add support, so they all know were in this together. We both know we could be looking for night watchman jobs, in 90 days if we fail."

"Makes good sense to me," Toni said. "Then let's get started now," suggested the Lieutenant. "The chief will be looking for fast action."

Lieutenant Daniels picked up his phone, and got Tom Granger on the first ring. "Tom, I need to see you, right now." Toni was sure he had agreed. For any of his faults, Granger always had respected the chain of command. Daniels hung up and turned to Toni.

"I'd like to take the lead in this initial discussion, if that's OK with you," he asked. "Tom needs to know why we want him...no that's not right, why we NEED him on the team."

"Fine," said Toni, "whatever you think will get the most out of him, I'm for that."

About that time, there was a sharp rap on the door and the Lieutenant waved Granger in. Tom's eyes darted to both of them, unsure what the meeting was about. He could only wonder if another complaint had been lodged against him...but he'd tried so hard to obey the rules.

Lieutenant Daniels began, "First, Tom, there are only a handful of people who know what we're going to talk about now, and it has to stay that way." Granger nodded his acceptance of that. "Tom, we've been handed a real crisis situation here. And the person who is doing the handing is Chief Perez."

Tom's eyes grew wider. Daniels continued, "Detective Ramos here, has been assigned to develop a task force to investigate, arrest, and convict the first known serial killer we've had in this city since I've been on the job. She's been given 'carte blanche' for personnel, overtime, equipment, computer time, you name it, the chief's handwriting couldn't be more clear."

Detective Ramos has agreed to the assignment, under one condition. She wants you on the team, I want you on the team and that means, Chief Perez wants you on the team."

Daniels proceeded, "Our first meeting is at one this afternoon, two hours from now. We'll be in a conference room on 7, which will be the HQ of the task force. That will raise fewer questions than if we meet in this office."

"What do you say, Tom?" the Lieutenant asked. He took the bait. "If the chief wants me on the team, how can I say no?" Tom answered.

"Good," Daniels said with a smile. "Now, no information to anyone in the department other than the fact that you've been given a 'special' assignment', and you have to hand all your other active cases over to me for reassignment, once we determine the other team members."

"OK, see you at 1," the Lieutenant announced while standing up from behind his desk. The lieutenant extended his hand and it was accepted by the strong, weathered vise grip of Tom Granger. A deal had just been made.

"And thanks, Tom," Toni added. "I know we haven't always seen eye-to-eye, but we need you." "We'll be fine," Granger replied, "Let's just catch the bad guy," he commented, leaving the office.

"OK, the Lieutenant said, "you handle Rosa, Billy, and Starr."

"No details, just invite them to a confidential meeting directed by the chief. You'll find that using his name will open a lot of doors for you."

Lt. Daniels added, "I'm going up to the Internet Technology Department on the 4th floor, to handle the temporary transfer of Adrian Keller, from her boss, Pete Moore. Then I'm going to ask Dr. Alexander to give us 30 minutes of his time today, as well, in briefing the group. They may have questions which we aren't qualified to answer."

"I'll check in on our resident profiler, as well, couldn't hurt," he concluded.

Toni sat back and began to make her calls to the three others she wanted in the group. Billy had already volunteered, although he didn't know for what. Rosa, and Starr were eager to be included in a special assignment. Of course, they didn't know what was involved, yet either. They would soon learn the pressure a case like this could bring with it.

Toni was very happy when they agreed to the upcoming meting. Rosa was a veteran cop, who was extremely detail oriented. Starr Jones was young, smart, and very attractive, which helped when she was questioning men of the opposite sex. She didn't try to use it, she didn't have to. It was just there.

Four

The conference room was large enough for 20 people. Toni's permanent task force members totaled six, including herself. It seemed like they were meeting in a football stadium, with all the wasted space.

Toni mentally categorized them, and thought she had struck a good balance. She itemized...Billy, the cowboy, Rosa, the expert on predators, Starr, the up and comer, Adrian, the I.T. expert, and Tom Granger, the enforcer.

Today they had the additional presence of Lt. Don Daniels, Dr. Alexander, and Dr. Felipe Zuniga, full time psychiatrist and part time profiler.

Dr. Zuniga was some what of a dilettante, and had developed a reputation of being a little above the fray, so to speak. Every now and then, he would bless us with his presence and throw a few choice pieces of his opinion to the masses.

Toni gave the group the overview she had been privy to only 4 hours ago. Then she asked the Doctors to give their impressions, in order to get on with their other duties.

Dr. Alexander was first, and repeated the medical facts in the cases, dates and approximate times of death, cause of death, toxicology screen results, lack of defensive wounds, etc. Then he opened the floor to questions.

"Any sign of petechial hemorrhage," asked Starr? She is smart, Toni thought. Dr. Alexander explained, "A petechial hemorrhage is a pinpoint of blood leaking from the tiny capillaries around the eye. It is an indication of asphyxia, by strangling or smothering."

The doctor continued, "To answer your question, no. And there is no question as to the cause of death."

He concluded, "We're still examining the marks on the skin and spine, and we have narrowed down the list of possible murder weapons to three or four. I hope to have something conclusive by this time tomorrow."

Rosa Padilla was the next to question, "Isn't Rohypnol illegal in this country?"

"Yes," the doctor replied, "but so is pot, speeding, and robbery, things you all know happen everyday, here in beautiful San Antonio."

He finished, "It's illegal to import it, but it's legal as an everyday sedative in South and Central America, Mexico, as well as many European countries." Rosa noted, "That's an angle to follow," and it was one of the first words written on the whiteboard, at the end of the room.

Dr. Zuniga was next up. Believe it or not, he was wearing a heavy wool jacket with leather elbow patches, and held an unlit pipe between his teeth. Toni knew, it wasn't the cool weather, she'd seen that same jacket when it was 105 degrees, he wanted to look the part.

He rose, with his copies of the Murder Book pages containing his comments. The Murder Book was an archive of everything about each individual murder investigation. The Detective in charge, in this case, Toni, had to ensure that this book contained every single medical examination, expert opinion, crime scene photo, victim background, or credit check, interview...in other words, the entire case.

Dr. Zuniga began reviewing his notes, while speaking. "We know that the average serial killer is a white male, aged 25 to 55, lives alone, usually fairly intelligent. In cases of young, female abduction, we can usually speculate he has above average looks. What disturbs me about this individual is that these messages indicate a sense of entitled retribution. Someone who things that he is the avenging angel, so to speak, out to right certain wrongs, in the society."

Billy raised his hand, "I've been wondering if this gang reference and revenge motivation, isn't just some diversion, you know to get us chasing our tails, while he keeps killing more women. Fifty bucks says when we find him, and we will, it'll be a psycho killer, with a mommy problem."

Dr. Zuniga replied, "That was the next paragraph in my analysis, officer, if you'd taken the time to read it." Billy cringed, as Dr. Zuniga continued, "Serial killers with above-average intellect, many times resort to changes in M.O., victimology (choosing a different gender, every now and then), even a different murder weapon, but that's rare."

Dr. Zuniga added, "These days, with electronic mail, he nodded toward Adrian Keller, I would think the killer would continue to communicate, for attribution, that's what it's all about." He added, "But, they will, in some cases, add diversions from their intended path. They will do these things for the reasons that it will confuse us, and if they get caught, confuse a jury...what's the intent, the defense would ask?"

He finished, "In conclusion, we just have to rely on the averages, until we get more data. This is embryonic in its nature. We've caught this thing very early in the process. Bundy, Dahmer, Gacy, had already killed at least a dozen people before they were suspected, we need more data to narrow our motivational options."

"Anything else I can add?" No one spoke up, and Dr. Zuniga folded his opinion, handed it to Toni, and left the meeting.

Tom Granger, spoke out, "More frigging data. What he means is more bodies. That's what he wants." Toni nodded, "I agree that's what he meant, I don't think that's what he wants, though."

Toni started again, "OK, here are the assignments. We've got to start from the bottom up. Rosa, you are on the background detail. There's got to be more to this than meets the eye. These two young women must have something in common. If we can find out what, we can start to narrow our focus."

"Billy and Starr, I want you flashing pictures of the victims at the bars downtown., this afternoon, and again, with tonight's bar shift. Someone had to serve them a drink. Keller, you add the words 'gang', 'gangs', and justice, to the key word filter." "Already done," Adrian replied, "up and running as we speak."

Another sharp one Toni thought, proudly. We need people like that in all departments. People who are not just counting down their days till retirement.

"Tom and I will canvass the areas where the bodies were located, then double back to town and start asking street people if they saw anything unusual. OK by you, Tom?"

"Sounds like the right place to start." he agreed, "Just don't use the word 'unusual'. It's a synonym for downtown. Try 'out of the ordinary'." And they both laughed. That made Toni happy. A little piece of camaraderie.

She finished, "We'll meet back here at 8 am tomorrow. We'll have to prepare our progress for the chief by noon. Daniels will want to see it beforehand. Be thinking about what you want in it, and what you want to leave out. By that I mean, don't include speculation. We'll just be chasing our tails."

The meeting broke up, with the group preparing to leave, when Toni stopped them, "Look people, the media is going to get this soon. We can't be the leak, or it everyone's ass."

"More importantly," she added, "I can't tell you how much every extra day without the press spotlight will add to our chance of success in this case. We owe it to the victims and their families to be as professional and discreet as possible."

The group nodded to each other, leaving with perhaps a little more urgency in their step. The common thought was that if the answer was there, they would find it.

Five

By 2:30, Starr and Billy were on the River Walk, showing photos of the two victims to bartenders of the dozens of bars on both sides of the San Antonio River. There were themed clubs from *Coyote Café* and *The Republic of Texas* to *The Old Irish Pub*. One thing about the River Walk, they covered all the bases. Their questioning had one rule. When the bartender was a man, Starr did most of the talking, and vice versa. They had to play all the angles.

Luckily, it was a slow time of the day, and they accomplished their initial run in time to walk the few blocks to the more traditional "El Mercado" a collection of shops, bakeries, and the famous restaurant, *La Margarita* where sizzling fajitas were consumed by the ton, cerveza and margaritas flowed as deep as the river itself.

Opened by the Cortez brothers in 1941, it has now grown to include the finest in Mexican food with a Texas twist, and in the past few years had added an oyster bar. Having a "SAPD" badge allowed Billy and Starr to avoid the usual wait. However, it was a trip which produced no tangible results for the investigation. Just another busy place.

Billy said, "A killer would be stupid to come looking for his victims with all these eyes around, just plain stupid. There must be 300 people here including the outside tables."

Starr disagreed, "It's the first place I'd go. With all this commotion, who'd notice anyone or anything?" Billy conceded she had a point. But, La Margarita and the other bars in El Mercado had produced nothing, so far. They would return later that night, and also to the River Walk, to catch the night shift. Maybe they'd have more luck then.

Rosa had followed up on the employers of Mendez (Williamson and Brown, LLC) and Anders, (Cooper, Strudwick, and Estevez, Attorneys at Law). Both companies had commemorative photos of the young women in conspicuous places in their lobbies.

Private interviews with peers, subordinates, and bosses, in each company produced nothing negative. No gossip, no insubordination. Both were paid very well for their work, probably a little more than average. Hard to find and keep good help, Rosa thought, but not if you pay them just a little bit more.

Both victims had been young, single, childless, and had excellent employment records. She had checked their "police records" or better said, lack of same. Rosa ran their State and NCIC profiles. Angela Mendez had a speeding ticket over 3 years ago. She was doing 47, in a 35 zone, on Blanco Road. No resisting, no alcohol, paid her fine by mail...nada.

Paige Anders, was as clean as a whistle. Both women's credit scores were over 720, with very little debt. Talk about your model citizens. What was she missing, Rosa asked herself? No one is this perfect. Something had to match up somewhere.

Tom and Toni spent quite a bit of the afternoon at the scenes where the bodies had been discovered. Both of them thought this was a waste of time. Everyone agreed that the killings had occurred elsewhere. The bodies had simply been delivered there.

But, it was part of basic police work. Even though the forensic team had spent dozens of man hours on site, they had to be there. They had to start at the earliest part of the crime, of which they were aware. The quarry yielded no results. Mendez' body had been rolled over the edge of the pit, and had fallen only about 6 feet to a ledge. It might have gone unnoticed until decomposition began, but a nearby work crew had seen a pack of stray dogs tearing at the blanket the woman had been wrapped in.

Yes, each one of that construction crew had been questioned at the scene by the first responders, with no luck. No one saw anything...again.

Toni and Tom next travelled to the west side, Huebner Rd. This was a heavily travelled thoroughfare. The body had been found about 20 yards off the edge of the road, wrapped in a black blanket which was unnoticed at night, however it was easy to spot up against the vegetation, the next morning. A state trooper had called it in, once he determined there might be a body inside the blanket.

Toni reviewed her notes. She said, "Tom, it says here that her body was in a ditch. But the ditch is right near the road. The taped off, outlined area, is a long ways from the ditch. Her body had to have been dragged through the ditch, and another 20 yards to the bushes and the cottonwood trees."

Tom looked at his notes. "You're right," he agreed. "First lets call the officer who discovered the body. That reference to being found in a ditch was made by Dr. Alexander, not a cop. He could have been ad-libbing." To complicate matters, they didn't have the Murder Book with them which contained the crime scene sketches and photos. As per regulation, they had left the book back at the station.

"You see the situation?" Tom asked. "Not really," Toni replied. "just a mix up in semantics, a verbal blunder," she said.

"No ma'm," Tom observed, "the doctor's comments don't mean anything to me. That's not what I'm talking about. I mean the job. Even with a smallish, 125 pound body, which is all dead weight, it takes a helluva strong man to drag that body through the ditch and another 20 yards through the brush. And we'd know if it was really was dragged. Would'a left a trail through the grass," said the old hunter, "but there isn't one." Toni observed, "A really strong man, if she was carried."

"Unless it was two men," Tom concluded. "O shit!," said Toni, "Please, let me have a simple one. Just once, a simple one. This could change things."

"I guess visiting the scene is really a good thing," laughed Tom, "but I guess we're done, here."

"I'm glad we both agree on that," Toni said. "We could have missed something big." Toni continued, "Lets go downtown, Tom, and look for something out of the ordinary."

The local street people hadn't been able to tell them that they'd seen anything unusual (for them), especially since most of them didn't even know what day it was. The trip was necessary, but unproductive.

You can question these street people all you want. They either are faking, or actually have, dementia, mental disorders, bipolar minds, or something.

Six

The next morning at 7:30 am, Toni checked the Murder Book. Tom and Toni had been right in their assumption. Dr. Alexander had simply said "found in a ditch" when the body was actually found 52 ft. 4 in. from the south side of Huebner Rd., against some heavy undergrowth.

The photos taken at the scene showed no trail where the body had been dragged, and it would have. The ground was moist from an earlier rain shower. Tom had been right, it would have left a trail.

They pondered over this discovery for awhile. How far should they let this new finding take them. If they weren't careful, it could derail the entire investigation, just because something didn't fit in with the rest of the clues. They decided to tread lightly on this possibility with the task force, and not carry it any further, outside the group.

The entire team was present for their 8 am meeting, by 7:45...everyone was antsy. Even Billy Cheatham showed up early, and it looked like he got some sleep last night, Toni thought.

Toni went to the whiteboard. Actually it was two boards which had been pulled together. The headings were, "Death Date", "Victim", "Vic. Info", "Medical", "Cause", "Message", "Crime Scene", "Observations" and lastly, "Links". A total of nine categories, so far.

Death Dates, Message Dates, Medical, and Cause, had been filled in for the two cases. There weren't enough similarities or clues on the board to convict even a confessed killer, and it was bothering Toni. There had to be something, even this early in the investigation, which they were missing.

Toni asked, "Rosa, you did the backgrounds, what did they have in common?"

"Lots," Rosa replied, "lots." Toni looked anxiously. Instantly, Rosa burst her bubble. "They were perfectly clean, no arrests, no ex-husbands or jealous boyfriends, no bad debt, no drugs, great work records, and clean credit."

Toni gave a deflated look around the room, as if searching for an answer. Rosa gave her a glimmer, "I would almost say too clean." She continued, "Even in your early or mid twenties, you have to have made a mistake somewhere, but not these two."

"And," she added, "they went to different gyms, shopped at different stores, everything is a dead end...one friggin' speeding ticket on Blanco Road, by Mendez, that's it."

Toni asked, "When was the ticket?" Rosa replied, "Three and a half years ago."

"Nothing since then?" Toni asked in desperation.

"Neither has been cited for jaywalking or for spitting on the street," Rosa answered with frustration.

The team went through the other categories. Nothing from the bartenders, no breaks from the crazy street people, and Adrian had no new email messages, of course there were no new bodies, yet.

Toni lowered her voice to the group. She said, "We have an anomaly, a clue which doesn't fit in with our working theory. We must keep this within this room. I've told no one. If it comes out before I say, heads will roll."

Toni asked Tom Granger to share with the group, the possibility that more than one man had perpetrated the crimes.

Tom gave the group the recap on the observations he and Toni had made at crime scene number two, careful to add that it was all a far-fetched conjecture at this point in time. It still could have been a strong man, or the murderer could have used a wheelbarrow, or some other method to transport the body to it's point of discovery. At this juncture, anything was still a possibility.

This is why they had decided not to include that potential clue in the report to the chief, or even to Lt. Daniels, not at this stage of the investigation.

Team serial killers were about as rare as hens teeth, and flew in the face of conventional wisdom. They didn't want to be ridiculed by experts like Dr. Zuniga, without something more concrete. This hunch would remain in the room.

About 10 am, Lt. Daniels dropped in on the group to see if the initial day had gleaned anything useful. Toni was realistic when she said, "Don, even Dr. Zuniga said we were way ahead of this, compared to other serial murder crimes."

"I want to solve it yesterday, too, but it's not going to happen overnight just because we want it to. We haven't found much, but we have eliminated a great deal, in a very short period of time."

She shared with him the backgrounds, or lack thereof especially of any commonalities, for the victims, and gave him a recap of their half-day old investigation. She thought that organizationally the team had covered a great deal of ground in a short period of time, and hopefully the chief would see that.

She did get a commitment from the Lieutenant that he would go to the narcotics division, before meeting with the chief, and request help with who might be selling or better yet, buying Rohypnol. This was one concrete lead which they needed to follow up on.

Before the lieutenant left, it was decided by all of them that today's report would be an update of who was on the task force, and the preliminary ground which had been covered. The killings had not been linked by the media as of yet, so the outside pressure had not yet begun.

Toni outlined the tasks for today, assignments would be for Adrian, to add the key words, Rohypnol, and roofies, to the screening of key words.

Toni wanted Billy and Starr, to check with the bars, again. They usually worked three shifts. Who knew who might have been actually working the night of the murders? Bartenders and wait staff were always trading off nights for personal reasons. Their actual, written schedules, were meaningless.

"Rosa," Toni asked, "dig deeper into the companies who employed the CPA and attorney. What types of clients were in their lists which might match up?"

Tom and Toni were going to call parents, friends, and classmates of the victims. They had already been notified of the deaths, in the case of the Mendez woman, over a month ago, but who knew what they might have been missed in the initial interviews. Someone could have remembered something which they considered unimportant, at the time.

With all the grief and surprise involved, people go away, mentally. It's human nature, and Toni had witnessed it too many times. They go through a state of shock, denial, and then withdrawal. It's the way people cope, emotionally, with tragedy. Many times they don't think about a little something, which six months later, winds up breaking the case.

Tom would take the parents first, (he volunteered) then he and Toni would split the friends and classmates.

Seven

The Taker was proud of the jobs done so far, and the fact that the authorities were seemingly still clueless of how or why the killings had taken place. They knew what the emails said, but they wouldn't, or couldn't take that as an answer. Just like the old saying, "You can lead a horse to water, but you can't make him drink." Well, these particular horses were about to be taught a valuable lesson.

It was so simple. The date-rape drug was easy to come by. The method of execution left no clues, and the disposal was easy in a town as large as San Antonio.

Now the curveballs would appear. Timing, victims, but not method probably, would change. The police would still be scratching their heads when number three, and possibly numbers four and five occurred. When would they wise up? How long would it take?

It was good to be in control of a situation. It was priceless (like the commercial said) to be unpredictable. And pressure...they'd seen nothing, yet.

The Taker had played it so cool at work. Never asking for time off, never calling in sick, never causing any undo attention to a cause, or belief. That's how people got caught.

The Taker knew things the police didn't. And they were about to go for a ride. Friday would be a good night to go shopping. San Antonio was like a giant department store. So much to choose from. So little time. But wait, the police weren't in control of time, were they? No, The Taker had control of the timing, as well.

No, not at all. The authorities were simply witnesses to the retribution that was occurring. Once they figured out what was happening, the public would no longer be on their side...the masses would be calling for their collective heads. The sides would switch. The hunters would be scorned. The killer would take a bow.

That had a nice sound to it, and so appropriate that a smile briefly appeared. But that couldn't happen, not just yet. This was a war. A war which was long overdue. And The Taker was in charge.

Eight

The days were exhausting. But actually, it was just the beginning of the task force's real police work. Day one and two had been getting the squad together, organizing information, going back through the things which had been already investigated, studied, photographed, and theorized.

Days 3 and 4 had the emotional element of grieving parents and former friends and employees. "Why would anyone want to harm her?", saddened classmates, would ask. Better friends would admit "I had at least 3 classes a year with her each year at UTSA, but still didn't know her very well." Older acquaintances would offer, "She came to Mass every Sunday since I've been at St. Paul's, and that's been seven years."

In almost all of those conversations and scenarios, the people who were being interviewed kept asking why the police weren't out trying to apprehend the killer, instead of prying into the girls' personal lives. They didn't understand the investigation process. The public just wanted results.

Rosa Padilla had been grinding out the background checks and itemized credit histories on the victims for two days now, with exactly zero luck. Everything still came back with a big goose egg.

She decided that this cursory look at the victims had run it's course. She decided to re-visit the two companies which employed them. This time she wanted to find out what she could about the type of businesses these were.

Yes, there were law firms who did nothing but wills or probate, some specialized in consumer class action, or real estate, etc. The same could be said about accounting companies. Did they represent mainly other companies' interests, or did they do individual tax returns? Rosa thought this would be a good area to investigate. It could offer some similarities. Or, was she just grasping at air? Well, wherever this new tack took her, she was now convinced that the murders were not about the victims. It was something else.

The accounting firm of Williamson and Brown was located in a modern office-park area of about half a dozen 4-story glass buildings. It was situated well for business access, at the corner of Bandera Road and Wurzbach, just off the 410 loop.

She had decided that for both victims, she would just go to the top rung people. Owners knew where their threats may be. With that in mind, Rosa had eventually gotten through to both firm's senior partners.

She told them that she only needed five minutes of their time to close out her background check on Angela Mendez. No, she had told them, there was nothing new, just SOP, a couple of blanks to fill in before she could move on to more critical areas. No reason to tell them it was a fishing expedition, she thought.

Rosa arrived at the office park about 10:15, and went to the 3rd floor of the building she had visited earlier in the week. She presented herself to the receptionist, who was expecting her. Rosa waited in a nearby conference room, and in about 5 minutes was joined by Dave Williamson and Sharon Brown-Lopez. Their fathers had begun the business together about 30 years ago, Williamson offered.

After greetings were exchanged, Rosa again apologized for the inconvenience, though both partners said that they would do anything at all to help find the killer of Angela Mendez. They sat at the end of a large conference table, the two accountants leaning forward to hear the questions. This was an old interrogation tactic which Rosa particularly liked using on important people. She would speak very softly, inviting them to get closer, for better observation.

What she wanted, today, was something about the firm. She didn't know what, but there had to be a connection.

She began by asking for an organizational chart, Brown-Lopez picked up the phone and requested one be delivered to the room. No, the company was not thinking of selling out to one of the larger, multi-national firms. Yes, they were adding another office on the east side of town next year.

Rosa took a chance. "Do you have any international clients?" she asked. The both sat up, became rigid, and looked at one another for just a second. Gotcha, Rosa thought. Dave Williamson answered, "Well, we can't discuss clients," he said. "Of course not," Rosa calmly said back to him. "I'm not asking you to talk about an individual client, just do you have any international customers?"

"Well," he stammered. "I'm not sure we can get into that." Rosa now knew an area where they were sensitive. "No problem," she said. Rosa asked, "Do you have much business with the firms of the other victim, Cooper, Strudwick?" Williamson answered, "Not really, I just know them by reputation." Rosa said, "Last thing, were either one of you related to Ms. Mendez?" They said they weren't, but Rosa already knew that, she just wanted to end the meeting on a non-threatening note.

"Well, thanks, that wraps us up. Sorry for the second visit. I'll wait in the lobby for the company chart." Again they were all smiling, and as luck would have it, a clerk from HR came down with the organizational chart, just at that time. It was one who Rosa recognized from her prior visit. He volunteered, "I think I gave you this a couple of days ago, but here's another."

Williamson and Brown briefly looked at her and Rosa said, "It must have been in the package you had prepared for me. All of you were so helpful, it will take me days just to get through this company paper work. I'm sorry to be so disorganized."

Rosa excused herself to the elevator, got back in her car, and realized she had found something. Touched a nerve, somewhere. What she found, she wasn't sure. But she was trained to observe people's reactions. What she'd seen, or felt, in that conference room was more than a little out of the ordinary.

She drove off to do some thinking, over a breakfast taco with black coffee. She had gotten off to a late start today and missed breakfast. All the better to study what I might have found, she thought.

Her appointment with Cooper, Strudwick, and Estevez, wasn't until 1 pm. She drove to one of her favorite places, a mom and pop breakfast/lunch eatery, and took her usual corner booth. You just couldn't get quality like this in the larger restaurants. She was sure the tortillas were made by hand, this morning. Everything in this place was always a day fresher, and thus more enjoyable. And in this place you could linger, drink your coffee slowly, and think.

After eating she drove east to a little part of town called Kirby. This was another business-friendly location. The office complex was at less than ½ mile from I-35, I-10, and the 410 loop.

The law firm was located in another cookie cutter glass office space, you couldn't tell it from the CPA's building.

She again waited in a conference room, just off the lobby. The lawyers made her wait 9 minutes. Allen Strudwick and Domingo Estevez made their entrance, joining Rosa at the end of the table. Again, she apologized for the inconvenience. They both restated their willingness to go the extra mile to find Paige Anders' killer.

Rosa asked about the business. She was told that Mr. Cooper had been the original senior partner, but had retired several years ago. "We have a firm, which practices a mix of the law which primarily includes real estate, environmental, and a little estate law," Estevez explained. "No malpractice, class action, or tort, he offered, too many people do that already."

Rosa was taking notes, and asked softly, "Do you have an organizational chart you could give me, just so I can make sure my later notes are correct?"

Strudwick answered, "Of course," and picked up the phone to order one for her. As with the accountants, she already had a chart from her first visit, but she was stalling for time. "And, you said that Ms. Anders worked for whom?" Rosa asked.

"Primarily, Ed Blessing," Estevez interjected. "Like all of us at this small firm, she worked where we needed her at the time, but most often with Blessing, in real estate."

"OK," Rosa said, reviewing her notes, carefully. "Oh, I forgot to ask, do you have any international clients?" They both reacted just as the CPAs had. They quickly straightened their posture, looking at each other. Rosa beat them to the punch, "I know you can't discuss individual clients, I just wanted to know where your business came from." They didn't have to give her an answer, past the body language she had already seen.

Estevez answered, "Without checking the files, I'd say that 90% of our clients are from here in San Antonio, or the suburbs." Rosa pushed, "Do you do much business with the firms of the other victim, Williamson and Brown?" Strudwick answered, "No, not really. They have an excellent reputation, but we don't know them."

"That's fine," Rosa assured him, and simultaneously, the organizational chart appeared in a paralegal's hands, knocking on the glass door to the conference room. Rosa took the paperwork, and briefly looked at it. She looked up at the attorneys, and said, "I certainly thank you gentlemen for your time today. I'm hoping the city doesn't get billed your standard hourly rates," she said kiddingly.

They both were very demonstrative in their display of offering any and all assistance possible, without compromising their relationship with clients.

With that, Rosa thanked them again for their time, excused herself, and took the elevator down to the parking area. She had something. She didn't know what, but she had something there.

She could feel the tension caused at both firms when she inquired about international clients. There must be more than meets the eye, and Rosa was determined to find it.

Where to look, was the big question.

Nine

At the end of this, the 5th day, Billy Cheatham was glad to get home to his small condo on the north side, and pour himself a Corona, with lime. He was glad that it was Friday, this weekend he was off duty, barring major events, and his steady girlfriend of the past three months, Rita Estrada, would be over in less than an hour, providing him relief from the hell of the past few days, investigating a puzzling criminal.

Of course, Billy didn't advertise that he was seeing the beautiful Rita. For that he had two reasons. One, there was always the possibility of moving up or at least capturing the stray young girl on the prowl for a man with a gun. There were always plenty of those around in the bars and nightclubs of a town like San Antonio.

Two, Rita was the 6 pm news anchor person for Channel 13, KBOY, TV. She was a constant rabble rouser, he'd heard the saying, "if it bleeds, it leads" from her own mouth. But, it was such a pretty mouth.

Regardless, his relationship with her, or any other member of the media for that matter, would have deprived him of any "choice" case assignments. The San Antonio police and the broadcast or print media were not the best of friends.

He would be hung out to dry, and feel lucky to be covering events at the Elks club, or recording births at the San Antonio Zoo, if his superiors found out he was sleeping with the enemy.

No, tonight would be all play, and no work, as far as Billy Cheatham was concerned.

Rita rang his doorbell, and entered with the key he had given her, about 6:15. She had come over straight from her 30 minute news show, which aired at 5 on weekends (Friday – Sunday) like today, and 6, Monday through Thursday. She asked how his day was going and he replied with the usual, "Still plenty of bad guys out there to catch."

Rita had heard some whispers about two killings being possibly linked, and he answered, "Don't ask me, I'm only in homicide. Besides, remember our little rule about not crossing the line between jobs?" She did remember it, never planned to honor it, but dropped it, for now. Rita knew that getting inside information from Billy was only a matter of time. And, this wasn't the time.

She had brought some T-Bones over, red wine and a bottle of Billy's favorite tequila, so she was prepared for the full court press. Dinner wasn't over till 9, with the tequila first, medium rare steak, baked potato, wow!

The meal was wonderful, and they were just in the throes of a very physical dessert, when his cell phone started vibrating. "Leave it," she said, "I'll make it worth your while." He did, and she did.

About an hour later he checked his messages. Toni had left him a voicemail at 10:15. "Tell whoever you're screwing, that tonight will be the last time you'll have a dick, unless I hear back from you in the next hour. We've got another one! The Taker has his third victim."

Billy bolted out of bed, halfway sober, and returned the call, "I'm on the way, where to" he asked. "San Pedro and Bitters, over by the Airport, she said, 10 minutes from you, be here in 5, or else."

Billy jumped into his jeans, pulled on his work shoes (Nikes), and said, "Rita, gotta go." "Not without me, she screamed." He didn't have time for this. He grabbed an ice pick from his kitchen drawer, and flattened 2 tires on Rita's BMW, before pulling his Audi out around her car in the driveway, heading for I-410.

"I'll call you later he yelled back. You'll get a scoop if there is one," he promised. "Chinga tu madre", she screamed as he headed down the exit from his condo. She was left standing there in his bed sheet. Oh well, Billy thought, they were both users.

Cheatham arrived at the scene. Strobe flashers reminded him of a rock concert. His badge finally got him in to the area where the forensics team was, and met up with a flustered Toni Ramos.

"Who the hell were you...never mind, you couldn't have prevented this, the M.E. said the victim had been dead for 2 hours, maybe 3 maximum."

"Same MO, he asked?" Toni just nodded her head. About that time, a news chopper 13, KBOY, started circling the area. "How did they get here so fast?" Toni questioned. "We use different radio frequencies for this case." Billy shrugged his shoulders.

Starr Jones was the next to show up at the crime scene. "Why don't you get rid of the chopper,?" she asked Toni. "How do I do that?" Toni asked in return. Starr said, "Simple, just call the captain, tell him to notify the FAA about the helicopter. It's probably in restricted airspace, we're right next to the airport for Christ's sake." Two minutes later the chopper was gone.

The victim's ID said that his name was Dan Lewis. His business cards said that he was a "Private Banking Consultant" for The Alamo Bank and Trust, here in San Antonio. His license said he was 25 years old. He was Caucasian. His clothes looked expensive, but dirty. There was a musty smell from the body.

It had to be the Taker, Toni realized, but this time a man, and only a few days after the last killing. This violated all the standard patterns of what the experts thought was typical serial killer behavior.

Some of these psychotics were driven by urges, some were on a lunar cycle, what was this about? Tom Granger drove up in his Dodge Ram 4x4, pulled to the side and walked toward Toni, flashing his badge to all the other crowd control cops in the way. He was met with the same set of basic questions as Toni.

Something wasn't right. This was so far out of the serial killer parameters, that it seemed staged. Toni said to everyone gathered. "My office, 8 am, Billy, call Rosa and Andria, tell them to meet us." Nothing more they could do until forensics, and crime scene gave their reports.

Billy drove home. No Rita. Her BMW was gone too. Bed sheets and blanket in the middle of the lawn, front door wide open. At least it was a safe neighborhood, or until tonight it was.

Toni drove home to her little rancher. It was in an area called Castle Hills, north side, just a few minutes north of the I-410 loop. It was what was called a "patio home" here in San Antonio. Built on a slab foundation in the late 1960s, it was about 1800 square feet, 2 bedrooms, with a 1-car garage.

She had updated the kitchen in the 4 years she had owned it, replaced the carpet with wood, and created a little garden, and pond in the tiny space which passed as a backyard.

The lots, as well as the homes, were small, so the neighborhood was populated by empty nesters, mostly retirees, and young professionals. This produced a very quiet neighborhood, which was great for Toni and her erratic work schedule. She grabbed a Corona from her barren refrigerator, and went through the back sliders out to a small lanai. This was her spot to relax and think after a long day at work. Tonight, "worry" edged out all the other contenders for her thinking capacity.

Toni had never been married, and wasn't in a close relationship with anyone who she could trade ideas with. So it was just her, and her 3-year old terrier, Buster.

Suddenly, the bell rang, and it startled her. Buster started barking. She never had visitors. Toni grabbed her Glock 19 from the belted holster hanging over the living room chair, and approached the door. She looked through the peephole. There stood Tom Granger. She put the semi-automatic in her back waistband, and opened the door.

"Tom," she questioned, "what's up?" "You know," he started, "I used to be able to go home, have a Scotch, and talk to my wife, Angie, whenever we got one of these weird cases. But since the accident, (his wife of 24 years had been killed in a head collision with an illegal alien) I don't have anyone to listen to me, or discuss theories with."

Tom added, "I though you might be in the same boat as me, so I took a chance." Toni was surprised. Not surprised that he needed someone to help him think out loud. But, that he respected her opinion enough to come to her. Toni said,

"Tom, you're reading my mind. Two heads are always better than one. I don't have any Scotch, but will a Corona work?"

"Sure," he said, "thanks." She invited him in and Tom quickly made friends with Buster. She said, "Let's go out to the patio, I was just starting my 1st beer, and my 1st thoughts."

They sat beside the wrought iron table and started bouncing some ideas around. "Well," Tom started, "I thought we might think this through in reverse." Toni questioned, "What do you mean?"

Tom stated, "Instead of banging our collective heads into the brick wall looking for who committed these killings, and I think we can agree that it's the same person or persons," Toni was nodding, "Let's see if there are some people or groups, who we can eliminate from consideration."

"Makes sense," said Toni. "We know this," she continued, "It wasn't the gangs, why bring more attention to themselves, it wasn't random, the victims, maybe, but the profile, no, all yuppies, sure to make the 6 o'clock news. People don't think much when a street person is mugged, or a crack dealer gets shot down, but young adults like this, that's different."

Tom added, "And despite the 'roofies' it wasn't sexually driven, plus the vic's all had their jewelry, id's, and credit cards, with them, so it wasn't about money, and the first two, most probably, this latest one as well, had squeaky clean records, so it wasn't about drugs, and we had no ex-husbands or close sexual acquaintances, which leaves out the jealous spouse or boyfriend criminal. So what the hell are we left with on this case? We're going nowhere, but if I had to think out loud, I'd say congratulations to us. We've eliminated 95% of the reasons people murder other people. Gangs, sex, money, drugs, jealousy, gambling, and personal disagreements."

"Which leaves us with two things," Tom deduced.

"A real psychotic, anti-young successful professional. Someone who thinks he or she should have been as successful as these three were, and is making a statement."

Toni asked, "What kind of statement?"

"A statement that being young and prosperous means very little if you're dead," he interpreted. They thought about that for a couple of minutes. "But, I don't think so," Tom added.

"There's one, very scary possibility, which I was hoping we'd never have to consider."

"What's that?" asked Toni. Tom looked her dead straight in the eyes. "Every now and then they say, 'what you see is what you get'." He explained, "We might have someone who has a grudge against the gangs...just like they say in their messages."

"And this Taker, is cold, calculating, and won't stop. I don't want to be quoted on this, but it could be a cop, or ex-cop. The crime scenes are almost too perfect. The one clue we think we found, that the body wasn't dragged, wasn't evidence, it was the absence of evidence. Think about that, for awhile. The Taker, thinks the authorities, that being the cops, DA's office, and the court system, are failing them."

Tom added, "And you know what I think. I think that in his eyes, he's right. This person sees no progress by the police in controlling the gangs, in fact, they are growing."

He continued, "I know every cop and DA in the city is busting their collective humps trying to put these gang thugs away, but it's not working. We're handicapped. We have to work within a set of civilized parameters, the gangs don't."

"And neither does the 'Taker'," said Toni.

Toni said her thoughts aloud, "Heaven help us if we have one of these murderers who think they are justified, and righteous. Nothing is more dangerous than a zealot, a person with a cause, who is willing to risk everything for that cause."

Toni and Tom thought and discussed for another 30 minutes the possibility he had just presented. Could it be that. What you see is what you get? "Well, I think we have some ideas, more than we started with, anyway." she said. "Let's see if we can punch some holes in that last one, keep rolling it around in our heads," Tom finished.

She finished, "Maybe something will show up different on this one. Give Dr. Zuniga the more data he was looking for. Let's call it a night, Tom, what do you say." He answered, "Good idea," he said. "But don't give too much weight to that last possibility I mentioned. I'm no psychic." Tom said his goodbyes to Toni, and Buster, and left.

Toni knew one more thing. Tom Granger was no fool, either. If he didn't think the "zealot" theory was plausible, he wouldn't have mentioned it. He'd been around the block a few times, but this one had him stumped. At least he was smart enough to admit it.

She let Buster outside for his last 5 minutes before bedtime. She kept speculating about the case from all angles in her mind. When that offered nothing of further value, she let Buster inside, locked up, checked all the doors and windows and went to take a much-needed hot shower. Toni turned the security system on for the first time in months.

She finished her Corona, and turned out the lights. Sleep was an elusive prey. She just had to wait until 8 am to get a better handle on things.

Ten

The eight o'clock meeting was somber, to say the least. It became much worse, in the first five minutes.

The email message Adrian Keller brought to the 8 am meeting was crystal clear. It read:

Why Have you been Focusing on me, and not the Gangs?

I told you what I wanted, and you Ignored me.

Right now, you may have a "Task Force" Looking for me.

Shine the Light on the Gangs, and I will Disappear.

Keep Hunting me, and others will Disappear.

What do you Choose?

Your time is getting Shorter...The Taker

There was no denying the source, or authenticity of the message. There was also no option but to put this in the chief's daily report. There was no getting around it, he wouldn't like it, but that goes with the job.

Toni was most fearful of one part of the message, "Your time is getting shorter." Toni knew what that meant, and how the chief would take it.

She and Tom Granger shared a cautious look after the message had been read. The other parts of the email were predictable, maybe not the reference to a possible task force. But, people knew more about police work today, with CSI, NCIS, and other similar criminal shows on TV.

Every investigation into a pattern killer, had a task force assigned to it. But, so soon? Maybe she was reading too much into it, Toni thought to herself.

The forensics and crime scene people agreed on many things. Cause of death, was a similar murder weapon, the body had been dumped out of a car near San Pedro Av., probably on Bitters, which was much less travelled. There was no evidence, yet, determining whether it was 1 or 2 people involved or whether "roofies" had been in the tox screen.

Toni went to the whiteboards and filled in all the data available. There wasn't much there to narrow down the search, except that the gender had changed.

"Rosa," Toni opened, "I spoke to the Lieutenant on the way in. He looked like he spent the night here" Toni continued, "He said that Captain Bernardo had already called the President of Alamo Bank and Trust. He's an old friend of the Captain's".

"He's expecting you this morning, even though it's Saturday, after our meeting. You'll get full cooperation from him, the man's co-workers, and the human resources department. Check his complete background too. I don't think you'll find anything, but I know you'll be as thorough with Dan Lewis as you were as with the first two," she concluded.

Toni then addressed the group. "Dr. Alexander asked for five minutes in front of the task force, so he'll be here any time now." She asked "Does anyone see anything different about this case, a new angle, an idea other than what's written on the board?"

Rosa said, "If there is something, we'll find it, you can be sure of that." Toni said, "OK, unless we get something revolutionary from Dr. Alexander, we'll proceed with Lewis as with the first two."

"Starr and Billy, go back to the bars with the photo of Dan Lewis, all three shifts. I know that upsets you Billy, but just take one for the force," she said, trying to inject some levity into a horrible situation. At that moment, Dr. Alexander knocked, stuck his head in the door, and asked, "OK to come on in?"

"Sure," said Toni, "what's the new info?" The Doctor noted, "It wasn't my office that found it. Forensics has been on this in conjunction with the FBI, and we've found what we believe to be the murder weapon."

He had their rapt attention. "Well, no, not "The" murder weapon, but what was used to kill the first two, and probably the third victim as well." He reached into a brown bag and came out with a pair of "garden shears?" asked Starr. "Not actually, he said, limb pruners, but watch." He looked around the room and saw a wooden pointer beside the whiteboard.

"Ah, perfect," he said. "The thickness of the cervical spine can vary, depending on the age and morphology of the subject, calcification, or anomalous deposits which transverse the spinal cord itself, however ..."

"In English, Doctor, please," asked Toni. "Of course," said Dr. Alexander, "If this pointer is the spine, this limb pruner is the weapon, he placed the pointer inside the pruner, and you have a groggy victim facedown on the floor" he pushed the handles together, quickly...'SNAP' went the pointer, in a split second, "It's relatively simple." The group was stunned into silent revulsion, they all went pale. "What?" said the doctor, "the marks match, this is it."

With that, the doctor left, puzzled why this news wasn't better received. They just didn't appreciate all the work behind this, he thought.

Toni knew that despite the sickness felt by all those in the task force, now they knew basically, what the murder weapon was. Which was a lot more than they knew 30 minutes ago. And it was her job to get the group past that demonstration and back to their earlier assignments.

Tom Granger stood up. "Toni, can I say something to the group?" he asked. "Sure," Toni said, hoping it wasn't about their theory developed last night.

Tom said, "I've been on the job for a long time." He turned to Starr, "Girl, you were in elementary school when I started. But you've turned into a heck of a cop. You're smart, smarter than me, and I'm proud to be a part of the team with you."

"You now see why they wanted me here...because of shit like this thing we witnessed today. I've seen it all, and what shock value can do to good cops."

"It gets under your skin, it makes you want to kill whoever is doing this. But you can't do it. We can't come down to this sicko's level. We have to retain our professionalism."

Tom continued, "My first year on the job, some crack head put his twin baby girls in the microwave, one at a time, and pressed 'ON' just to see what would happen. The door was closed, so you couldn't hear them scream. I got there when the mother called us."

Tom continued, "There sat a skinhead with a big grin on his face. He looked me in the eye and said, 'whatcha goin' to do about it, pig?' Three other cops pulled me off the guy. He almost walked free because of me, and my anger. I would have eaten a bullet if that had happened. If my emotional irresponsibility had let that animal to get off, I could have never lived with myself."

"So what I'm saying is, forget about what you saw here today. The best way to honor the dead is to catch the 'doer'. Get evidence, look everywhere, be a pro. Don't be like I was."

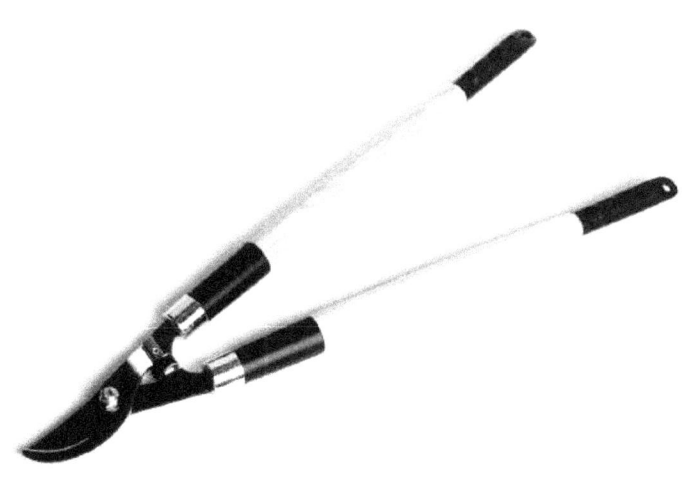

Eleven

Rosa Padilla walked into the main office of the Alamo Bank and Trust. The bank was located just off loop 410, which was where many large corporations such as USAA, had their national headquarters.

Her appointment was with Mr. Eugene Bloom, and within 3 minutes of showing her credentials to the receptionist, and asking for Mr. Bloom, Rosa was escorted to the 4th floor and entered an outer lobby where Mr. Bloom was already standing, waiting for her. Mr. Bloom was one of those men who fit their profession. In the old days, before "Google", if you had looked up the word "banker" in the dictionary, Mr. Bloom's likeness would have appeared in the margin beside the definition.

After condolences were shared, Rosa asked the usual questions, and received the answers she was expecting. Yes, he had a perfect work record for the 4 years he was employed here. In fact he had been a summer intern, his senior year at college at the University of Texas in Austin, 80 miles north up I-35. No, he had no disciplinary problems, but she could check with HR, to verify. He had very few social friends here at the bank. He didn't know anything about his outside friends or lifestyle, but he still lived at home with his parents, here in San Antonio.

Toni asked for the HR contact's name and wrote it down. Cindy Lopez, she was next on the list. Mr. Bloom called her, and said she could see her whenever, and for however long it took, if it would help find the murderer.

After thanking Mr. Bloom for his time, Rosa was escorted to Human Resources at the other end of the hall on the 4th floor.

Cindy Lopez was an attractive blonde, obviously an Anglo married to a Hispanic man. The absence of a wedding band told more about her. She was very helpful and extremely competent. She didn't ask her assistant to get the files for her former employee, she dug them out herself.

This was impressive to Rosa, especially being a female. Rosa had been sent for coffee in the "old days", and had always bitten her tongue. Now she didn't have to. It was a new world. The victim's HR files were more of what she was expecting, no problems. A great work ethic, an almost perfect attendance record, etc., etc.

Rosa thanked Ms. Lopez for her time and walked to the elevator bank. She looked back into Mr. Bloom's office, a question surfacing in her line of thought. She stuck her head into the door. He happened to be sitting at his desk, the door open. "Mind if I ask you two more questions?" she asked. "Anything," Bloom answered, "anything at all."

"Do you do any international business?" she asked. Bloom stuttered and stammered, looking at the ceiling, "I'm not really sure," he said. "You know we're a home grown bank, but we do have 8 branch locations in south Texas." Well, Rosa thought, that answered that question. The same as the other two firms.

She continued, "Well, my second question, may be personal, but how did you know that Dan Lewis still lived at home?" Rosa asked, "That's something you wouldn't usually know."

"Oh, sorry. I assumed Captain Bernardo told you. I've known "Danny" since he was born. The Lewis family, Ron and Glenda have been neighbors of mine out in Bourne, for years, and before that, closer into the city, on Callaghan Road. Also, the Lewis's were among the original founders of this bank. It's public record, I'm not talking out of school."

Rosa took a minute to catch her breath. "Former Governor Lewis?" Mr. Bloom answered, "The very same. Would you like me to set up an appointment with Ron and Glenda?" he asked. "No thank you," Rosa answered, "I have more to cover before I get to them." This case wasn't hot enough, already, she thought?

The next thing Rosa did was straight out of the unwritten book of police procedure and protocol. She called her boss, Toni, who was at the scene where the body had been discovered, with Tom Granger.

"Oh shit," Toni exclaimed. "Now I'll have the chief riding shotgun in my squad car...no he'll be driving, I'll be in the street." "Rosa, handle this one exactly like the others...to the letter. Credit check, bank accounts, NCIC, etc. I want no stone left unturned because of whose son he is," or was, she corrected herself, mentally.

Toni then called the Major Crimes Section. She was told that Lieutenant Daniels was not in, and no one knew when he would be back. She knew this was hot enough to track him down. Don Daniels answered his cell phone on the 1st ring, "Daniels here." Toni started to get to the point, and he said, "hold on, I can't hear you, I'll go outside for a better signal."

The Lieutenant got back on the line, "I couldn't talk in there, I'm with the chief, the Captain, and the former Governor, at the Lewis residence. I couldn't call and warn you because the chief stopped by my desk, said 'get your coat', and we've been together every minute since then."

"Let me tell you, former Governor Lewis wants a crucifixion, and my palms hurt. How do yours feel?" Toni didn't answer, she knew heads could roll, and soon.

"Let me tell you something else I've found out since I've been here. Dan Lewis was gay. The governor wants it classified as a 'hate crime' and wants to call in the FBI."

"No," said Toni, "not the Feds. "That's exactly what we don't need right now. We would waste 2 days, just bringing them up to speed on what we do, and don't know."

Lieutenant Daniels responded, "Thank God the chief has talked him out of that...for now." He told Governor Lewis that the 1st two victims were straight females, but get Rosa working on that angle, if she isn't already." He said, "I've got to get inside. I'll verify that the 1st two were straight...tell Rosa to make it so," and he hung up.

Toni called Rosa back and gave her that new slant on the case. Rosa said, "Well I talked to two guys who had dated Mendez, and one who went out with Anders. There was nothing serious in either case, but both men said the women had normal, heterosexual lives." Toni let out a big exhale and texted the Lieutenant, so he could see that sexual orientation was not a motive.

Toni then sent out a text to the task force, there would be a meeting at 3:00 on the 7th floor. Time to regroup.

Tom and Toni had found nothing at their scene, and when they returned to the station, Rosa was huddled behind a computer. She looked up, and making sure no one else was around, said, "Same as the others, clean records, good credit, yada, yada, yada." But, she added, I'm working an angle I'll talk to you about later, if it has any merit."

The 3 pm meeting was a rehash of all they had uncovered that morning on the victims...zilch! Starr and Billy had struck out in the bars, and after Toni's call, they made the rounds at a few of the most popular gay bars, with all three photos...nothing.

Adrian Keller had added the word "gay" to the filter, got 180,000+ hits in 30 seconds, she took it off, but put on "Governor's son", nothing came back. Rosa was intent on finding the link. She had two girls in their teens, and as a single mom, had her hands full. Her husband had been killed, two years ago, in Iraq, by an IED.

Tom looked at Toni, and she nodded. Toni got up from her chair and began. "This is a team, so I'm asking for some participation here, some ideas, someone to shoot down what I'm going to say, which stays in this room, this room only, understood?" They all nodded. "Tom and I were talking, trying to piece this thing together. We, it was Tom's idea, decided to use reverse criminology on this case. We started by eliminating people or motives who probably didn't commit the crimes, rather than look for who did. Just a different slant on things," she said.

She continued, "despite the 'roofies', the killings weren't about sex, agreed? Everyone nodded. "The victims all had money, jewelry, id's, and credit cards, found on the bodies. That eliminates money, OK?" More nodding from the group.

With the first two, most probably this latest one as well, we found extremely clean records, so it wasn't about drugs or gangs. There were no ex-husbands, or fiancés, with the first two, we'll have to dig some more on Lewis, but I'm betting his situation would be the same. I don't think being gay meant anything. So that eliminates the jealous lover angle."

She looked at Tom, "Did I leave anything out?" he shook his head. "So," Toni summed up, "kudos to us. We've eliminated

95% of the reasons people murder other people, those being gangs, sex, money, drugs, jealousy, gambling, and personal disagreements, agreed?" Again, the group couldn't argue.

"Which left us with two possibilities...one, someone who is jealous of successful young professionals." Starr spoke up, "Sounds weak to me."

"It did to us, as well," Toni said. "Well where, exactly, does that leave us," asked Billy. Toni replied, "One other option, and it's definitely not good, how did you put it, Tom?"

Tom replied, "Number two, is that sometimes, what you see is what you get. We may have someone who is exactly who they say they are. Look at the messages on the emails. It could be someone who holds a grudge against the gangs, and thinks that the Cops, the DA's Office, and the Criminal Justice System, isn't doing their job. I would admit, from the outside, it sure looks that way. Comments, anyone?"

Billy burst out, defensively, "Hey man, we're doing everything we can. Not just us, but the Gang-Related section, the Narco Squad, we spend a lot of money trying to take the miserable creeps off the streets."

"How's it working?" Tom asked rhetorically. No answer was needed. The problem had grown, and no progress had been made. Toni begged, "Please someone shoot this theory down. The last thing we need is a zealot."

No one had any better ideas.

"OK," Toni said, 'at least we have a new avenue to pursue." "Adrian," she turned to the I.T. expert, "can we filter people or families who have been victimized by the gangs, with the perps going free?" The woman answered, "Of course."

Adrian answered, "We start with all the gang related killings in the past, say 5 years, and then filter them by those who were exonerated, pled down to a lesser charge, were cut loose on a technicality, etc., and we have a list, but..." Toni interrupted, but what?

"It's like putting the word 'gay' on the filter, it's going to be a big list."

Toni said, "Do it anyway, it may help us connect the dots, eventually." Of course, Toni knew, there was no eventually, in this case, ex-Governor Lewis would make sure of that.

"Now," Toni said, "we still need to do the same things we've been doing. But, with even more intensity. Background checks, interviews, the whole course of police work. We let I.T. come up with possible matches, but it's only a list which can help us once we come up with a suspect."

"If we find suspects, and they are on the list, we can pressure them. It increases the amount of credible pressure we can put on a suspect ."

"However, and I want you to put this as strongly as I can. Just because the suspect is 'not' on the list, makes them no less a suspect, remember that."

Toni added, "I hope that all you realize that the chief, the Captain, and Lieutenant Daniels were at ex-Governor Lewis' home until about thirty minutes ago. If you thought the heat was on before, it's just been turned up, big time."

The group all left the meeting to continue their assignments, probably more shocked and confused than ever.

Tom stayed behind. "How did we do," asked Toni. "We have a great team," Tom said. "Once they get back on the streets, which is where they belong, they'll be fine."

"Besides," Toni added, hopefully, "Rita, is working on a hunch. She wants to pursue it further before she gives it any merit, so at this point, it's more of he same. Basic police work."

"Right," Tom answered, "but with the chief and the former governor looking over your shoulder."

Twelve

Sunday's, *San Antonio Express News*, had 4 inch headlines:

The "Pruner" Takes Third Victim!

Yes, they had the story. It was mostly accurate. They knew the type of murder weapon, which is where they came up with "The Pruner", and the way the victims had died.

They knew the names of the three people murdered, and the way the criminal had communicated through the Internet. They knew the gist of those messages. They had a great many of the details. Probably the work of ex-governor Lewis, Toni thought.

Governor Lewis believed that turning up the pressure would help get his son's case solved more quickly. He had good intentions, but he was wrong. All this did, Toni thought, was turn the investigation into a circus, and put the killer on notice, that he had killed someone of some notoriety.

Not to be outdone, the lead stories on Channels 3, 10, and 13 that morning, was "The Pruner." The chief was to hold a press conference at 1 pm. The task force, Lieutenant Daniels, Captain Ramos, Drs. Alexander and Zuniga, and the chief, were to meet at 11.

The deputy chief, Fred Unser, called the meeting to order, no one had been late, pensions were a good thing.

"OK, he asked, "what do we have that the press doesn't?"

"Let me give a recap," Captain Daniels offered bravely. "The victims had nothing in common, except that they were all, successful young professionals who were murdered in the exact same fashion. All three of their arrest records, credit scores, lifestyles, and work history were spotless."

"Their social lives, besides Lewis being gay, were social, with nothing serious. Neither of the women had serious relationships, we're still investigating Lewis, but none that we know of, were heavily involved with another person."

The assistant chief interrupted, You can forget investigating Lewis, his family wants his sexual orientation to be kept out of it." Lt. Daniels answered, "We don't think his being gay has anything to do with the murder. But we'll investigate him, just like the others. If the chief wants my badge, I'm right here." The chief shook his head, "No, you're doing the right thing, keep it up."

Chief Perez added, "No special treatment, but we're not going to increase pressure on the gay community either. This man was a victim. I don't care about his sex, the bars he frequented, the men he saw, unless it adds to the investigation, period." Chief Perez' reputation just took a big positive move up with the cops in the room.

"Let the chips fall where they may," he added. "One more thing," he added, "I want those chips lined up, ASAP."

"Loud and clear," Lieutenant Daniels promised, knowing the chief's military background.

"Alright," the assistant chief said, "opinions from the experts." Dr. Alexander. Sam Alexander rose and started, " I think it's 100% that we have a serial killer. The pattern has not changed, just the timing has shortened. I am now in a position to say that the identical weapon was utilized in all three crimes."

"Dr. Zuniga," deputy Unser asked, "can you add to this?" The Doctor rose and said, "There are two things I can add. Both of which I have given to the task force, previously. One, most serial killers are apprehended between their 12th to 20th killing. We caught this early."

"It's of no consolation to the families who have lost loved ones, but being this proactive at this early point in time gives us a great advantage over those who finally apprehended Gacy, Bundy, and Dahmer. We can shorten the time span and number of victims killed here. We have a good start."

"And the second thing, doctor" asked Unser. "In reading the email communications," said Zuniga, "we could have an avenging angel situation." "What's that?" asked Captain Bernardo. Dr. Zuniga answered, "It's possible we have an 'advocate' with a cause. That is to say a person who thinks of themselves as the avenging angel, so to speak, out to right certain wrongs, in the society."

"What would that mean?" asked Chief Perez.

"That would be your worst nightmare," Dr. Zuniga answered. "This would be someone with a clean background, who believes that they, or their family has been victimized by the gangs, and not been given any justice from the law and judicial system. From the communications I've seen, that would be my best guess."

"Thank you Doctor Zuniga, said the deputy chief, "Captain Daniels, how have you dealt with this theory?

Toni made a career decision. "Please let me answer this question, after all I'm the closest to the case." If she had ever seen relief on Lieutenant Daniels' face, she saw it now.

"We've been working on this aspect of the case for a couple of days, now," she exaggerated. "We are compiling a list of everyone in the past five years who has been involved in a gang-related murder. We are emphasizing those who were arrested, but either plead down to a lesser offense, were exonerated by lack of witnesses, or changes in testimony, or who walked free, on a legal technicality."

Toni continued, "It's a big list, but we are placing great emphasis on it, so that when we find suspects who look guilty, we can apply a little more pressure on them, and add motive to the list for the DA's department. "However, and it's been my call, just because they are <u>not</u> on that list, doesn't mean we don't treat a suspect, like any other suspect."

Chief Perez commented, "I like the way you think, Detective, I believe you are on a good track. Suspect everyone, but prior perceptions of inadequate actions by law enforcement or the judicial system, can add to our case." No one dared to repudiate the chief. And Toni was right.

The meeting was adjourned. Lieutenant Daniels came over and said, "I'm happy, and I'm mad. You bailed me out, with the chief. But, why didn't you tell me about this theory?"

"Tom and I just developed it at the crime scene last night. We discussed it with the group only hours ago...it's only a theory. I didn't want it to get in the way of good, solid police work."

"So I had a few hours to discuss a 'hair-brained' theory with you, and didn't...shoot me. It'll probably be easier than another one of these inquisitions," she said. Daniels replied, "I would kiss you, but that would be harassment."

At 3 am, Carlos Ruiz, 2nd in command of the "Bloods", was on his way home to his crib on Castroville Road, just south of Commerce St. in Downtown. He saw a drunk. A very large man, but a drunk, nevertheless, trying to unlock his Lexus, dropping his keys, fumbling under the car for them.

Carlos was alone, for a change, but decided this was just too easy to pass up. At the least, he would have a premium car he could take to his chop shop, and if he were lucky, the drunk had a Rolex, credit cards, and cash on him. Carlos pulled in behind the Lexus and got out with an innocent helpful, attitude. He asked, "Esse, anything I can help you with?"

The drunk mumbled, "My keys, my keys." Carlos said, "Let me help you, homie," as he pulled the 12 inch pipe out of his back pocket. The drunk turned, he had a Colt 45 caliber, semi-automatic, with the end of the gun barrel inserted and duct-taped into an empty 2-liter cola bottle. The man pretending to be drunk said, "And I've got something for you, homie."

The big man fired, the bottle absorbing almost all of the sound, but none of the power of the 45 caliber, "hydra-shok" bullet. The round entered Carlos' body the size of a nickel and exited his back, the size of an orange.

The assumed "drunk" grabbed his keys, collected the spent brass, and drove home, all within the speed limit.

The next morning, Monday, at the 8 am task force meeting,

Adrian Keller delivered the latest of The Taker's emails. "This came in at 7 am," she said. "The filter ID'd it right away." She presented it to the group on a slide which simply said:

See How Easy That Was?

One Night, One Less Gang Leader.

Why Can't You Do That?

It Will Save a Lot of Innocent Lives.

The Taker

"Who got killed?" Asked Toni. "Billy, call the Gang Squad, I want to know what happened." Billy came back ten minutes later. "One of the chiefs of the 'Bloods', Carlos Ruiz, got himself killed early this morning."

"The squad figured it was gang related. His body and car were found just south of Commerce. From what the guys in Gang think, it looks like a 357 or 45 to the chest. I asked them to put a priority on it, and said it came from the chief. Otherwise the case would have sat on someone's desk for awhile."

Dammit, thought Toni. Another curveball. She called Lieutenant Daniels, and asked him to come up to their meeting if he had 5 minutes. He was there in 3.

Toni shared the email, and what steps they'd taken with the Gang Squad, forensics, and crime scene. They had put a rush on it, using the chief's name, without tipping their hand that it was probably connected to "The Taker."

Toni added, "Don, in discussing this with the group, we believe that this connection between the gang leader and The Taker, should not be revealed to anyone, especially the press."

Toni continued with her thought, "Yes, we can advise the Doctors involved and keep the chief in the loop, but it could be something of an ace in the hole for us. When we bring in a suspect, it could be that this murder, and it's connection to the others would only be known by the actual murderer. It might also help weed out false confessions, which I hear are growing by the hour."

Lieutenant Daniels thought about it for a moment, then said, "I agree. I'll tell the chief, and Captain Bernardo, to get their blessing, but I think it's a very good idea. Who knows?" He said, "Maybe the 'Crips' will want a little retaliation."

Toni faced the group. "It sounds more and more like that avenging angel we didn't want, just became our reality."

The rest of the day, Rosa's job was to delve deeper into the life of Dan Lewis. Dan was openly gay, not a closet variety. He frequented the upscale bars and men's clothing stores. His bills were paid on time, and his bank account was modest, especially for the son of an ex-governor.

Billy and Starr spent most of the day visiting Dan's favorite clubs, and once the management saw that the cops were there, not for harassment, but to find Dan's killer, they were most supportive.

Unfortunately, their support didn't produce any meaningful clues. No one knew of any serious, or recently ended relationships he had. Starr said it best when they reported in to Toni. "Dan Lewis was a gay, male carbon copy of the first two victims."

After a long, tedious day on the job, it was agreed that the five of them would make a last pass through the bars and clubs with photos of the women in hand. Tom and Toni would cover the River Walk, Billy and Rosa, El Mercado, and Starr, the jazz clubs.

She remembered that the search of Angela Mendez' apartment had on it's inventory sheet, several cd's by Thelonius Monk and Miles Davis. Not much to go on, but better than nothing.

Billy and Rosa were still striking out in El Mercado. Having Rosa with him helped, but these businesses were always being hit by INS raids, their overall cooperation was usually zero. Tonight was better, but no one remembered anything.

Toni and Tom Granger had more of the same. Some people thought they might have seen the women, somewhere, but young, pretty females were everywhere.

Starr walked into a club named *The Blue Note*, and was immediately "hit on" by two guys hoping to score. Their hopes evaporated when Starr pulled back the edge of her sports jacket to reveal a SAPD badge.

"But since you've been so friendly," Starr asked, "have either of you seen these women?" she said as she placed the photos on the table where she sat. Well, of course they hadn't, and beat a hasty retreat back to the barstools they had previously occupied.

Starr worked her way past the glances she was receiving from other men in the room and approached the bartender.

He was a veteran, "How can I help you officer?" he asked, without hesitation, "Name's Monty."

Starr laid the two photos out for him. He shook his head, but remarked, "This one I might have seen." he said pointing at the snapshot of Angela Mendez. "I might just be saying that because we don't have a lot of Hispanics who come in here. Mostly 80% blacks, the rest, Anglos. She's not a regular, but you'd have to ask my partner, Darius, he works the late night shift usually, but he's in Houston on vacation for a week."

"Tell you what," he offered, "leave me your card. I'll have him call you when he gets back." I'll just bet he will, thought Starr, as she slid her card across the table. Monty asked, "You got a cell or home number?" She answered "Just have him call the number on the card, they'll find me." Typical, just typical, she thought, and left the club to hit the next one on her list, *The Dew Drop Inn.*

Starr struck out there as well. No results to show for her efforts at any of the 8 jazz clubs she visited. She could have had several dates, if that was what she was looking for. But, she had a nice off and on relationship with a young car salesman, and was off the market in her own mind.

The next morning's briefing of the special task force was a compilation of the failures of the previous night. No one had made any progress with the photos. They had visited dozens of the most popular clubs, with no success. The five cops plus the I.T. person were all at dead ends.

Toni yelled, gruffly, "Billy, get ballistics up here, now. I want an update on the bullet that killed Carlos Ruiz. Tell them the chief's waiting for an answer." Toni asked Rosa, "On the victim's credit card statements, were there any places in common that these people went to frequently?" Rosa replied, "Just like it was the first three times you asked me, no."

"I'm sorry," said Toni, "I feel we're just chasing our tails, here, asking the wrong questions." Rosa said, "I don't think we're working the other half of the equation."

"What do you mean?" Toni asked. Rosa continued, "We still have to visit all these places and find the killer. Someone out there has seen them together, and we'll eventually find that witness we need. We just need a link."

"But," Rosa said, "Toni, early on, you asked me to see what common clients these companies had. Now we have three companies. A law firm, an accounting corporation, and a bank, she added. If we could get a list of the major clients of the three, and cross reference them, we won't necessarily find the killer, but it will give us a basis for alerting other firms who have the same clients. Somehow, I just feel that the commonalities behind these companies are just under the surface."

Just then, there was a knock on the door and Bobby Adams walked in with a bullet in a plastic evidence bag. "What've you got for us, Bobby?" she asked. Bobby grinned and replied, "It's a 45 ACP, Hydra Shok, in pretty bad condition. The only reason we got this, Doc says, is because it missed the sternum. A through and through, hit the victim small, broke 2 ribs, came out his back, fist sized, glanced off the street and lodged in a vehicle on cement blocks about 50 feet away. Otherwise it'd be gone."

Toni noticed Adrian's wonderment at the jargon. "Now Bobby, would you explain the terminology to our I.T. person here? She might never need to know, but just maybe," Toni said. "Sure," Bobby said, since he was feeling like a celebrity, "The bullet was a 45 caliber, American Colt Pistol, or ACP, and was a Federal brand, utilizing a type of round Federal calls 'Hydra Shok'."

"It's basically an enhanced hollow point which upon entering the body, mushrooms, causing the maximum damage possible, and a 45 is a powerful weapon, not accurate over 20 feet, but right up close, it'll stop a grizzly…" "That's quite enough, Bobby. I'm sure that now Ms. Keller has been educated on the 45 ACP."

"Thanks for coming, I'm sure there was no brass found." Bobby said "No, but I had something nagging me, so I checked it out." "OK," Toni said, "If no one else here is up to it, I guess I'll take the bait, what?"

"It would never hold up in court, bullet's in bad condition, but I checked the records and I think I found a match." Toni's and the rest of the task force leaned forward in their chairs. Bobby continued, "I'd say it's 90% that this bullet came from a 45 we had stolen out of the police evidence room last spring."

"Shit, again," Toni exclaimed. She put her face in her hands, and stayed quiet for 30 seconds, while those around her were moaning about yet another hurdle to jump. Billy was going on about how it couldn't be a cop, wouldn't be right to start looking there either. They'd have to bring in IAD…Toni stood up and barked at the group in front of her. They all started yelling their opinions. "Stop! Stop the quarreling, now." Toni yelled. "Tom Granger, what did we just hear?"

"Conjecture," he said. "Conjecture, that the man said would never hold up in court. Simply put, he's an expert, and he couldn't swear under oath that it is the same gun." Toni looked at the task force. "Exactly. Which means we heard nothing, nothing at all. We start accusing the force of involvement, I don't know about you, but I'll never make it as a bartender. I'm not saying to ignore it, keep it in the mix, but go no further down the road with it."

"Now, Rosa, I'm going to the lieutenant and see if we can get our legal department involved. Even with the 'juice' from the former Governor, it's probably going to be nearly impossible for us to get these three firms, especially the lawyers to, divulge their client lists to us. Their attorney-client privilege is sacrosanct, but we've got to try."

"I think we have our best chance with the bank, even maybe with the accounting firm, if the bank gives up it's list. As long as we stay low profile with it, Governor Lewis may be able to give us an entrée, there."

"We've got to stay proactive. Has anyone visited the gyms used by the victims?" asked Toni. "No, Starr, that's for you. You can go in workout clothes, register as a guest of the deceased. Pretend you don't know they are dead, it'll start the conversation."

She looked at Cheatham, "Billy, I want you to go to the other end of the spectrum. Visit the cheap, sleazy bars. Places you wouldn't want on your credit card or ATM statement. And I don't want to see any of these lap dancing receipts for reimbursement, either."

She asked, "Tom, please check the pawn shops, see if anyone has bought or sold a 45 caliber semi-automatic in the past 30 days. After that, check the state firearm sales records for a 60 mile radius.

"Now, Adrian, you add 45, Bloods, Crips, and automatic to the key word list, and stay tuned for excessive chatter on the Pruner. Maybe we can find out where the leak came from.

 "Lastly," Toni said, "Rosa, you stay on the backgrounds. I want to know what color socks Dan Lewis wore. But most importantly, I want to know what these three companies have in common. You're right. It has to be there."

Toni ended the meeting. "Now, unless there's anything else, I'm going to go throw up, eat three Altoids and go see the Lieutenant about getting our crack legal department involved."

"After that, I'll catch up with Tom, checking the gun stores, looking at ammo purchases, and digging for I don't know what, yet."

Thirteen

The next two days were consumed with even deeper searches into the backgrounds of the three victims. The daily news stories about "The Pruner" were still on the front page, but were now below the fold.

The pressure from the chief and the ex-Governor was constant. SAPD's request for help from their legal department, was literally a laugh in the face. Being attorneys themselves they knew that there would be no assistance from the law firm or the CPA practice, regarding client lists. The bank was dragging it's feet, citing "The Right to Financial Privacy Act of 1978", and the corresponding penalties for improper disclosure.

Basically, this law says that a governmental agency has the right to pursue and obtain a search warrant for access to a suspect's records, if, and only if, it is deemed to be an integral part of the criminal investigation, in other words, probable cause had to exist. This meant that the SAPD would have to convince a judge that all of Alamo Savings and Trust clients were suspects. Good luck with that one.

At the daily 8 am meeting the group looked downtrodden, tired, and frustrated, the same they'd all been since this case had begun.

Rosa began by enumerating all credit card and recorded purchases made by two of the three victims. The ex-governor had provided his son's last 3 months bills, he was paying for them anyway. Angela Mendez, the 1st victim had only 1 credit card, an American Express, and the monthly statement was lying on the hall table when her apartment was searched.

The department had received and served a subpoena for Paige Anders' Visa and Discover records, with both companies promising quick action. They should have those by tomorrow.

Billy had found nothing new in his repeated visits to bars of all types...county/western, Mexican, wine and Tapis, bars who only sold beer from "micro-breweries". He even had taken Rita Estrada with him to most of the Mexican places. They had reconciled, now, and he knew he wouldn't have a chance for information without her by his side. She was eager for the news scoop, so she was glad to play along.

Tom found no unusual transactions from the pawn shops for a 45, semi-automatic. It could have come from anywhere. As for the ammunition, the Federal hydra-shok cartridges were sold in 39 locations within the city limits, alone.

Starr had interviewed the staff from the gyms which the two women frequented. Paige Anders was a zealot for the weights and the "spin classes." Angela had been into boxing, and martial arts. She also held a brown belt in Judo.

Toni added, "So both these women, would have the ability to put up a pretty good fight," and got nods from around the room. "If she hadn't been drugged," she added.

Adrian had nothing new from I.T., which was the first good news to be presented, this morning.

Tom asked, "What about the 3rd car?" Toni had issued BOLOs (Be On the Look Out) for the vehicles owned by the victims. The Mendez car (BMW 325) and Lewis SUV (Porsche Cayenne) had both been located in Gypsy parking lots (not city lots with cameras) in the Downtown and River Walk areas. They'd been poured over by the forensics team with no results. It was very likely the murderer had not been inside either one, but they covered all their bases. Paige Anders' Jeep silver Cherokee was still not accounted for. "Nada," Toni answered, "but it'll show up.

Tom guessed, "It's most probably in 1000 little pieces right now. One of them is probably disguised as an ashtray, is my guess," which caused some much needed laughter from around the room.

Just then, Lieutenant Daniels stuck his head in the door and said, "Turn the TV onto Channel 13, right now."

The remote was closest to Starr, she turned it on and flipped to 13. Billy shut his eyes and listened.

"This is Rita Estrada with breaking news in the case of several murders attributed to a serial killer, formerly nicknamed 'The Pruner'. Channel 13 has come into exclusive knowledge that this person calls himself 'The Taker' and that a 4th victim, a reputed gang member, by the name Carlos Ruiz, was killed by this person, who previously murdered 3 young professionals here in San Antonio."

"Although the method of killing was different, unnamed sources say a large caliber handgun was used, the serial killer has contacted the San Antonio Police, and accepted credit for the killing."

"We'll have a complete, in depth report, on this exclusive story, featured on our 6pm show this evening. This is Rita

Estrada, reporting for KBOY, Channel 13, where you always get the news first."

The task force sat in stunned silence. The one thing they had hoped to keep from the media, was now public knowledge. Someone had talked to the press. If it wasn't a member of the task force, who was it?

Fourteen

The Taker was overjoyed. The press would magnify the spotlight on this Ruiz case, and now the cops would have to divert some of their resources to an altogether different crime, different M.O., and have to spend time interviewing people who wouldn't talk to them. It would be a nice diversion, all for nothing. That was part of the fun The Taker had. Watching the police work for meaningless reasons. It's a control thing.

The anonymous tip had been called in to the station which had the largest audience in the area. By tonight, the other media outlets would have picked up the story from their sources, and it would be the headline in tomorrow's *Express News*.

Billy used his short lunch break to call Rita Estrada's private cell number. "What the hell was that all about?" he demanded to know. "If you won't keep me informed," she said, "I have others who will. Now get over it."

Lieutenant Daniels called Toni over after the "news break", around 2 pm. He said, "The boys on 7 are getting restless, they want some progress. Do you have anything I can give them, anything at all?" he asked.

"Not yet, she said. We're about half way through developing the list of people involved in murders by the gangs who went unpunished. But look at the numbers, we begin with 400 cases in the past 5 years, eliminate the gang on gang killings, the family disputes, the ones who were convicted, the jealous spouse, and we're down to 150. Now we've got to follow up on how many of these were prosecuted and convicted of murder 1 or 2. That's where we are today."

Tom Granger knocked on the door, "Sorry, but they just found the Anders girl's Jeep." "Great" said the Lieutenant and Toni at the same time. "Where was it?" Toni asked.

"On the south side, just off Pleasanton," Tom replied. "The crime lab crew and forensics are already there." A cruiser spotted it due to the BOLO. They been on the scene for about 30 minutes, now. Lieutenant Daniels looked at the phone, as if deciding whether to call the Captain. No, he thought, I'll call him on the way. "Let's go, you two are with me," he said.

In 15 minutes, they arrived on the scene. He did call Captain Bernardo on his cell phone, and promised to keep him updated, hourly. The crime scene had been taped off, dozens of citizens craned their necks in an attempt to see what, they weren't sure. Three TV trucks were already on site, and a helicopter was hovering, overhead.

How did they beat them to the scene? Toni wondered. An SAPD tow truck awaited the OK to bring the Jeep into impound. Jimmy Rollins, leader of the crime scene investigators walked over to the Lieutenant and held up a baggie. "Look what I found on the back floorboard," Jimmy said to Daniels. There was an empty glass inside the baggie.

"Then what are you still doing here?" asked Lieutenant Daniels. "Get in your car, drive it directly to forensics, yourself. Give it to Paul Rosales, by hand. Be sure he signs for it, to keep the 'chain of evidence' intact. Tell him, the chief wants this at the head of the line. Tell him if he has a problem with that, call the chief. He wants results, yesterday. Now, go, and if you have an accident on the way, that glass better not break." Daniels turned to his fellow officers. "We may have caught a break," he stated. "Now if there are prints, and if that person has a print on file, we may have something."

Toni gave her assessment. "Maybe I've been around Granger too much," she started shaking her head, and elbowing Tom Granger in the ribs in a "just kidding" gesture, "but this seems awfully convenient."

"No witnesses, no hair or fibers, no physical evidence so far, nothing under the nails of the victims, and the creep leaves the victim's car out in the open, with a glass in the back floorboard? It just seems too convenient to me."

"Is that what you think as well, Tom?" the Lieutenant asked. Tom replied, "I've gotta tell you, it crossed my mind. But, let's play the hand we were dealt, and see where it leads us."

At 4:30, the Jeep was finally towed to the SAPD impound area. It was not left outside in the elements, however, it was put in the garage. It would be inspected again, by a second crime scene crew, looking for anything that was missed on the first examination.

"Let's call it a day," Toni said, "We won't know about the prints until tomorrow, anyway, and everyone is beat. Eight am, as usual, on 7," she said. "I'm with you," Granger said, and they drove to the Nueva St. headquarters.

From there, The task force all went home for some much-needed rest. Vince Lombardi, the great coach of the Green Bay Packers, said it best... "Fatigue makes cowards of us all."

Well, Toni didn't know about the "coward" part, but she knew that people thought more clearly and made better decisions, when they were rested.

Toni had an old college girlfriend coming over tonight. Theirs was not a stressful relationship. Toni and Rhonda Fleming, had been casual friends since high school, and roommates at UTSA. Rhonda was the type of person Toni could be comfortable with. They didn't have to impress each other. They had one thing in common which also made them close.

That was the men, or better said, the scarcity of men in their lives. They hadn't gone out of their was to discourage traditional relationships. Their commitment to their chosen career paths were enough. Being a police detective not only intimidated many possible suitors, but it was also the 80-hour work week with unpredictable hours. Emergency calls had ruined more than one relationship for Toni. Go to a nice dinner, only to have the cell phone summon her to a crime scene in the middle of the entree. That was difficult to compete with.

Rhonda was kept busy, at about the same pace as Toni. She had three small boutiques. One was on the River Walk, the second store was at North Star Mall, the city's largest shopping center with Macy's, Saks, and a pair of 40-ft tall cowboy boots in the parking lot.

She had opened her third store in Austin, a 90 minute

drive up I-35, in Highland Mall, about a year ago and had store #4, planned in the new mega-mall on I-35, opening in 6 months. This would be the largest mall in Texas, six anchors, 200 storefronts, with an ice rink over an acre in size. It was predicted to draw shoppers from as far away as one hundred miles. It was named "The Heart of Texas". Her store would be a one-of-a-kind, just as her others were. She specialized in smaller sizes of designer clothing for juniors and women.

She had a few shoes and bags on the side, but her shops, appropriately named "The Collection" did 90% of their business in fashion forward dresses and smart casual attire, over half of her sales in sizes 0-6. A small portion of the demographic, but one who had a tough time finding the right clothes without going to New York or L.A. Rhonda was becoming a big hit in the fashion retail world.

Tonight, however, would be jeans, sandals, a t-shirt, and stir-fried Chinese. They got together at least twice a month. Tonight was Toni's turn, and she had selected the menu.

Rhonda came over at 7, with two bottles of pinot grigio, and the women decided to have a glass, and decompress on the small lanai off Toni's small backyard. As always, the best part of their friendship was that they never, ever, talked about business.

Both were big readers, time permitting, and they had an unsaid rule that they would try to read at least one book each month. Rhonda had read, and brought with her, a copy of a book titled, *The Art of Racing in the Rain* by Garth Stein. It was a feel good book, something which Toni needed right now, and would begin next week.

Toni's contribution was *Lean Mean Thirteen* by Janet Evanovich, the latest in the Stephanie Plum series. This was one of their favorite authors. Lots of laughs. They traded books, and without giving away too much of the stories, discussed portions of the novels, while they spent time in the kitchen making dinner together. This was another special part of their ongoing relationship. They both knew each other's kitchen just as well as their own. A big part of their friendship was based on the bonding which was shared through meal preparation.

After dinner, they had fresh, cut-up fruit, mainly nectarines, strawberries, and plums with vanilla bean ice cream, for dessert.

They sat, as they had in their college dorm, and shared thoughts on books, men and life. The conversation carried through the minor cleanup up in the kitchen, one of the beauties of take out dinners. After the kitchen was tidied up, and the friends had a last glass of Pinot Grigio, it was unfortunately time to bring the evening to an end.

Rhonda said she had an early morning appointment, with the salesperson from Georgio Armani, and gave Toni (and Buster) a big hug on the way out. Toni was alone again. But, with the exception of a very few people, she liked it that way. Toni settled into sleep wearing a *San Antonio Spurs* t-shirt, with Buster by her side.

At 6 am, her cell phone rang, with the familiar ring tone of the "Volga Boatmen" dirge, identifying the call as coming from HQ. It went straight to voice mail. It was Captain Bernardo. He liked to keep things simple. The message said "Call me, now." The hits just keep on coming, Toni thought.

She called the police department, and was transferred to Captain Bernardo's, office. It seemed they were working more hours, as well. Captain Bernardo, was cryptic in his message, but transparent in his conversation with Toni.

"Be in my office at 7:30," he said, "Lieutenant Daniels will be there also." Toni got out of bed, showered, and fed Buster. He stayed in the garage or the small backyard, when Toni was at work, using a small doggie door from the kitchen.

Toni put on her favorite blue suit (for good luck), with a white kerchief in the jacket's front pocket. She grabbed her badge and gun, and left the house at 6:45. She was going to be early, but maybe she could find out what the meeting's agenda was.

Toni exited the elevator on three, and headed for her desk. There were only a few people in cubicles and sitting on desks, and she had seen none of he task force members who she could ask, so she made the decision to take a chance that Lt. Daniels was in his office. Toni ducked across the hallway and saw Daniels with his cup of coffee, reading the morning newspaper.

"What's up, boss?" Toni asked. "I wish I knew" he answered. "It could be about this," he speculated. The lieutenant held up the morning edition of the *Express News*.

Toni had not see the paper this morning. She just tossed it on her front steps of her home, before getting into her car and heading to the office.

The newspaper had huge headlines which said "Taker Evidence." The photograph below the headline, had obviously been taken from far away, with a telephoto lens.

It was a little "grainy", but clear enough. The photo showed a very happy Jimmy Rollins giving Lt. Daniels a clear plastic bag which held a glass.

Well, now she was prepared for a butt chewing from none other than Captain Bernardo. She was hoping that the chief wouldn't be in attendance.

Toni and Don Daniels read the accompanying article, which was basically a re-hash of previous stories the media had run. The news departments from the paper and TV stations were putting on a "full court press."

Toni asked, "What could we have done? The uniforms kept the public at least 100 feet away from the Jeep. Some news photographer climbs up a tree, and we're to blame? I just don't get this."

Daniels said, "I heard the forensics team worked all night on this, maybe we got lucky." The lieutenant called down to the crime lab, and asked for Jimmy Rollins. "You just missed him. He went upstairs to the seventh floor, for a meeting. You want me to leave him a message?"

Lt. Daniels looked at his watch. It read 7:20. "We've got to go. Jimmy Rollins is in the meeting. He must have matched the print." On the seventh floor, it was quiet as well. Captain Bernardo was sitting in his office, and once he saw Toni and the Lieutenant, he waved them inside.

Jimmy Rollins was right behind them, with a gleeful look on his face.

"OK," said Bernardo. "Mr. Rollins, you've got a captive audience. Please tell me that these people and I, didn't waste our time by meeting you here at this ungodly hour."

"And, by the way, don't ever have the duty sergeant call me on my mobile again, at 5:30 am," he fumed.

The Captain ended his tirade and looked at Jimmy. "So, what do you have to share with the group?"

Jimmy started his presentation, "The glass was a mid-range small shot glass from Mikasa. Low lead content, probably sells for about $30. There was a small chip on the rim which could have happened at anytime, so that's no help. There was a residue of tequila in the bottom, we're trying to track down the brand as we speak."

Toni looked at her Lieutenant. They both knew that Bernardo was about to go volcanic. She saw him in her mind's eye, throwing Rollins out of the larger of the two windows in his 7th floor office, so Toni interrupted, "Tell us about the prints. Did you find some prints?"

"Oh yes," Jimmy said, "a man's and a woman's." Captain Bernardo rose from his chair, put both hands on his desk leaning forward, toward Jimmy. The vein near his temple was dancing and turning black, he asked "annnnnnnnnd?"

"We got a match on the man's print, still running the female's." Jimmy still didn't get it. "Oh," he said, "the man's prints came from," he was looking at his writing in his pocket notebook, "Oh, here it is, William David Cheatham. I still have to run it through the FBI's AFIS/IAFIS database, which I've sent them, with top priority, and we're going to need Captain Daniels' people to investigate his background."

"He could be a drifter, you never know. I'll keep running the female prints and let you know if we get a 'hit', and when the

FBI verifies my analysis, but I don't have any doubts."

The Captain said, "Good work Mr. Rollins, you may be excused now. One more thing, if that name comes out in public, tomorrow, or this time next year, I'm going to blame you, and everyone else, in your office. I'm going to shoot you first, then beg forgiveness from the chief. Do you understand, clearly, what I've just told you?"

"Absolutely, Captain, and no one in my office knows about this, anyway. I'll keep it locked in a drawer in my office." Jimmy turned, opened the door, and Bernardo said, "Close it behind you."

The Captain looked at both of the other cops in the room, and said, "I'm getting too old for this shit!" He continued, "The good thing is, Rollins doesn't know what he has. If he did, it would probably be painted on the walls of all the restrooms in this building. There are over 500 police personnel in this building. Rollins has probably never met Billy Cheatham."

Toni offered some of her and Granger's theory. "We get no evidence on 4 murders. No hair, no dirt, no fibers...a very smart animal. Then he dumps a car out in the open, a car which contains a glass with his prints on it."

Toni continued, "The Taker' is yanking our chain, he wants us to spend valuable time on Carlos Ruiz, then gets the media worked up. I think this is an attempt to do the same thing, we probably have a couple of days before the press gets another anonymous phone call."

Lieutenant Daniels chipped in, "Listen people, I've had my own disagreements with Billy Cheatham. But it was always about procedure, never anything more. He's a cowboy in more ways than one, but I can't see him doing this thing. I think we've got to focus on finding the real 'Taker', and not get bogged down on extraneous fishing expeditions."

Toni was more convinced than ever. She spoke up, "Well, Captain, we all know Billy's not The Taker, I'd bet my badge on it."

"You just did, both of you." Captain Bernardo said. "I've got a meeting with the chief. Unless he overrules, you've got till 5 o'clock this afternoon to completely exonerate Billy Cheatham. That's all the time I'm giving you. After that, we've got to let the story out."

The captain lamented, "If the press gets wind that we're covering up one of our own, instead of protecting them, the department will never be trusted by the citizens again. And, I couldn't blame them."

"Lieutenant," the Captain concluded, "I want two people to interrogate him, a man and a woman. And I don't think it should involve either of you."

Daniels asked, "With all due respect, Captain, we know him better than most." The Captain nodded, "You just made my case. I want people who can be objective with him. Plus having one of them being female, will unsettle him, especially if she doesn't know much about him. I want to find out for sure."

He concluded, "My recommendations for the interview are Tom Granger, who would interrogate his mother if he thought she committed a crime, and that black, young woman, Starr Jones. She's part of the task force, and will keep this quiet if we get negative results from Billy. I don't want anyone who we can't trust to keep it quiet, if he's not the murderer."

The captain continued his directive, "Another thing you might consider is to tell the task force that Billy is out chasing down an obscure lead. Tell them that Lieutenant Daniels is filling in today, to make sure we don't shrink the number of investigators. Plus these people are already in the loop, and we won't be bring new people in."

"If there are no more questions, I'm going to the roof and think about my future in this position, or possible lack of same. Then I'll go see the chief," he concluded.

Fifteen

The meeting broke up and Toni had to get her "ducks in a row." She sent a text to Tom and Starr, telling them to come to their conference room on the 7th floor, ASAP. She texted Rosa and Adrian Keller, directing them to come to Toni's office, not the 7th floor. She sent nothing to Billy.

Toni, Rosa, Adrian, and Lieutenant Daniels would pursue the investigation, today. Tom and Starr would use their conference room on 7, as an interrogation room. No one would think twice about the three of them in that room. But if word got out that they were using one of the official interrogation rooms, everyone would know that a policeman had come under suspicion.

By 8:15 all of the players knew their roles. Toni had the tech department place a video tape and recording device in the room, using the chief's name again (he could attend the interrogation if he wanted to, right?) and the wheels moved more quickly than usual.

At 8:30 Adrian and Rosa were sitting at Toni's desk on the third floor, waiting for her to arrive. Meanwhile, Toni, along with Lieutenant Daniels, Starr Jones, and Tom Granger, were sitting in the 7th floor conference room when Billy Cheatham walked in.

As soon as he saw the camera, he knew this was out of the ordinary...something was different. "What's up with the camera?" Billy asked. "We bringing in a suspect? I hope it's a good one."

As previously planned, Lt. Daniels replied, "We've matched the prints from the glass we found in the Anders woman's car. A perfect, 100% match." Billy was excited, "Great," said Billy, "lets go nail this sick bastard. It's about time we caught a break on this."

"The prints were yours," he said. "Yours, and another woman's, who we haven't identified, as of yet," Toni responded.

Billy looked shocked, and he collapsed into his chair as if he'd been shot. He shook his head, clearing the cobwebs.

"But I didn't kill her, no way, no freaking way." Billy's head was spinning out of control. His demeanor changed from happy to see you, over to the defensive, in a microsecond.

Lieutenant Daniels leaned toward Billy, and stated, "Billy, no one in this room thinks so, either. Just look at the camera, it's turned off, as well as the recorder. The public is always saying that we look the other way on internal police business. That we cover-up things which contain police wrongdoing."

Daniels continued, "Captain Bernardo, through the chief, has agreed to give us a day to clear you, or the information goes to the press and IAD (Internal Affairs Division)."

Daniels explained, "Turn the thing around, Billy. If it were my prints on the glass, and you were the Lieutenant, would you throw the glass into the river, without considering the possibilities? Of course you wouldn't, and neither can we. It's our job to see this through to the conclusion, whatever that might be."

Lieutenant Daniels continued, "Part of our own team, Starr Jones and Tom Granger, are going to do their best to clear this up, today, right here in this room. That's the best thing we can offer."

"Detective Ramos and I will be working to help clear you, also, and we will also assist in the 'Taker' case today. We've not mentioned your name to anyone outside this room as a possible suspect, except for the captain. The forensics people don't know the identity of William David Cheatham, from Adam, but they will soon, if we can't clear you today."

Daniels finished, "Now, Billy, if you are innocent, sign this permission to search affidavit, so Toni and I can search your home without getting a court ordered warrant, and causing undue publicity." Billy signed, without even reading it, he knew what it said. "I don't have my keys with me," Billy said. "We'll get in," said Daniels, "with no damage."

Toni and the Lieutenant stood to leave, but Billy added, "Thanks for cutting me some slack. I know you didn't have to. And I'll be as cooperative as I can be."

The lieutenant turned to his interrogators, "Tom, Starr, I want this thing cleaned up today. I'll meet you back here at 5." Toni and Daniels left. They heard the video camera turn on, after which he knew Tom or Starr would read Billy his Miranda rights.

Back at Toni's desk, Lieutenant Daniels brought Rosa and Adrian up to speed on The Taker case. Today, Rosa was going to keep digging, Adrian would look for some more keywords.

Home for Billy was a small, 2-bedroom condo on the

north side, just a few blocks north of I-410. It was on the ground floor of a small condominium complex, containing 4 buildings of 8 condos apiece. The Lieutenant "jimmied" the door in about 1 minute. Toni said, "I'm impressed." Daniels replied, "I haven't always sat behind a desk, and besides, this is like riding a bike, you learn how to do it once, you never forget." They went through the unit methodically, taking precautions not to make Billy feel too violated, if the glass turned out to be a set up.

Toni was surprised by the clean, well appointed condo. There was no *Viking* oven or *Sub-Zero* refrigerator in the kitchen, but it was obviously upgraded with granite countertops and custom cabinets. The rest of the place was equally nice.

Billy didn't have any expensive paintings, or Dale Chihuly glass works, but there were some nicely framed prints and furniture, which was well selected. Toni asked herself, What was I expecting, saddles for chairs, wooden boxes overturned for a dining room table, what? Toni thought, should I be surprised that Billy doesn't live like I envisioned an ex-rodeo person to live?

He had turned the 2nd bedroom into an office. This is where he had his department commendations, a computer, printer, and plasma TV. In a corner of the office was a treadmill, from which he could see both the TV and the outside.

At the end of 2 hours, they had zero, zip, nada. They went to a small Texas-styled restaurant, nearby for lunch. The Lieutenant had chicken fried steak, Toni stayed on her perpetual diet and had a Caesar salad with grilled chicken on top.

After they were finished with small talk, Lieutenant Daniels said that he wanted to return to the condo and give it one more hour. He wanted Toni to search the rooms he had searched, and vice-versa. They gave it another attempt, room by room, the kitchen cabinets, the refrigerator with the same results.

At 2:30 pm they were wondering what the interview with Billy had produced, if anything, when Don Daniels' cell phone rang. He answered it , "Daniels."

It was Tom Granger, another man of few words, "He's clean, boss." Daniels asked, "Are you sure?" Granger added, "Yeah, he was out of town when the Anders woman was killed. Get this, it was his Grandmother's 90th birthday, in Lubbock, with plenty of witnesses, Starr and I talked to at least 10 of them, individually."

Tom said, "There are only 6 hours while he was there which I can't account for, and Lubbock is almost 400 miles from San Antonio, each way." Granger continued, "There aren't many flights from Lubbock to San Antonio, and the shortest is 3 hours."

The Lieutenant said, "I sort of remember giving him 4 days of vacation time back then. When I get back, I'll check with the personnel records department".

"I already did," replied Tom Granger, "you signed the form." "Then where did the glass come from?" asked the lieutenant.

Granger told him, "He said he was with Rita Estrada, at his place, between 6 pm or so until almost 11, when he answered Toni's voicemail on the Dan Lewis killing. Starr called Rita, she corroborated Billy's story."

Tom added, "Even the fact that she left the front door wide open. She was some kind of P.O.'d at the time with Billy."

"So am I," said the Lieutenant. "That idiot. Now we're talking about Rita Estrada from Channel 13, is that right?" Granger confirmed, "The one and only". Lt. Daniels complained, "Surprises are getting more and more common."

"There's more," Granger continued. "Estrada said she'd come in and get printed to confirm that the prints on the glass are hers, if you give her first shot at the story when we catch the SOB."

Tell her, "I'll have to speak with the Captain." Daniels said, "Unless she wants to be a good citizen and come in on her own so I don't have to issue an arrest warrant. And this freedom of the press B.S. won't work in this situation. We don't want her sources, we just need to borrow her fingers for 5 minutes. We could even say she's a suspect or at least, a material witness. How would that play with the media?"

"Let me talk it through with the Captain," Lieutenant Daniels said. "We just might be able to use her to our benefit for once."

"Tom, get the word out to the team. We'll hold a meeting in the 7th floor conference room at 5 this afternoon." Lieutenant Daniels instructed. "There are probably rumors flying around, and we need to refocus and get back on point. I'll be back at the office in 20 minutes. Then, you, Toni, Starr, and I will go see the Captain."

Don Daniels then called the Captain Bernardo's office and the captain said to come right up when he arrived. He mentioned that Chief Perez would be sitting in, as well as legal and IAD.

After Tom Granger had given his findings to the group, there was a consensus that the murderer, who called himself The Taker, had attempted to throw a diversion at the task force. The killer had stolen and planted the glass, while Billy was investigating the Lewis murder.

Don Daniels said, "It worked, too. Four of us spent the entire day following up a worthless lead, but one which had to be investigated. Thank God for Cheatham's 90-year old Grandmother."

Daniels continued, "Just like killing that gang member," and by the way, Cheatham convinced Tom here, that the anonymous tip on Ruiz did not come from Billy. "If Granger believes him, I believe him. But, my point is that the killer is spreading us very thin. We may need another investigator. Think about it Toni."

Lieutenant Daniels asked the representative from the legal department, "Any progress from the three employers of the victims?"

The man from legal, Chris Davis, replied. "The Senior Partner of the law firm hung up on me. I think if he could have, he would have laughed, but it was their employee who was murdered."

Davis added, "The accounting company has strict rules, but said that if the others cooperated, they'd give some disclosure, due consideration. I think he knew we would strike out with the lawyers, so he wasn't giving up much."

"Finally, the bank is being squeezed by the ex-governor, we could get something there, but without the others it's worthless."

One of the lawyers stood up from the group and said, "If there's nothing else for me, I've got a ton of things on my desk. I really need to get to work on several, important, items. Is this it?"

The chief gave him a dismissive wave with his hand, and said, "That's all for the rest of legal, IAD as well," and they both exited the room, leaving just the cops to talk about the case.

Captain Bernardo was the first to speak. "What are we going to do with that woman from Channel 13, Estrada? I know we can get a court order or issue a warrant for her prints."

The chief replied, "We've had a rocky road with the media, as in most cities. The way I see it is we have three avenues."

Chief Perez had analyzed all the aspects of the dilemma. "Number one, we could drag her butt in here with a court order, charge her with hindering an investigation, etc. Two, we could talk to our 'friends' at the Express News and get a newspaper story in about her being uncooperative, try to shame her into coming in and volunteering, or Three, make the deal, give her a head start when we finally find this lunatic."

"I vote for number 1," said Captain Bernardo. "Haul her in here, alert the other media, give this Rita Estrada a taste of her own medicine." Daniels said, "I can't really disagree," "But we might be seen a bullies by other members of the press, which is something we try to avoid."

"I think we'd be viewed, by the public, as taking all the possible steps to solve this case. That's exactly what the public wants...results," added Tom Granger.

"Anyone else?" Asked the chief. "I want a united front on how we handle this. No divisive thoughts aired."

"May I say something, sirs?" asked Starr Jones. "Please do," said the chief. Starr continued. "I'm new at this, so I might be out of line." Captain Bernardo said, "That's why you're in here. You should always speak your mind. But, whatever decision we make in this room, the chief wants it to be a unanimous vote, no back-biting if someone didn't get their way, understood?"

"Absolutely", Sir. Starr continued. "Make the deal, give her what she wants. That serves several purposes, not the least of which is her friendly relationship with an SAPD officer."

All the men looked at her in puzzlement. "You want us to make the deal, give her the story first?" said the Captain.

"Yes," Starr said, "and then use her. Use her to get information out that will bait the killer. She can quote her un-named SAPD source to spread mis-information, when it's time to set the trap to get this bastard, oh sorry, chief, for the language."

Starr was concerned, "But my greatest fear is this. The Taker knew where Billy lived. He probably knows where each one of us in this room lives, and the other members of the task force, as well."

Starr continued, "We must to get on the offensive. Bait this psycho into a mistake. Having a credible person like Rita, can help us get a phony story out, when the time is right. Not now, but eventually we'll have an ace in the hole, so to speak. Otherwise, we'll be doing our jobs while looking over our collective shoulders."

"I like it," said the chief. "Anyone see a fatal flaw in this course of action?" There was silence. "OK," said the chief, and added "Make it happen, lieutenant."

On the way down to the 3rd floor, Lieutenant Daniels said, "Good idea Starr, and since you were the one who spoke to her earlier today, you call her, tell her we've got a deal, but we're not signing any agreement. We'll go to her, for the prints, in order to avoid publicity. The one condition is, that she has to keep this quiet. If it gets out, the deal is off."

Sixteen

The 5 o'clock meeting went off as usual. The group discussed the planted evidence. Billy stood up to offer his take on the situation. "First of all," he said, "if any one of your prints had been on the glass, I'd have reacted just the same way as the Lieutenant. We can't afford to ignore a clue, just because it hits close to home. So, no hard feelings or grudges from me, except my contempt for the killer just rose one notch, if that's possible."

Toni Ramos said, "Thanks for that, Billy. Some of us, have worked with you for a long time." She pointed out, "This person who calls himself The Taker wants us sniping at each other, it works to his advantage. One more thing. During the last few hours, we have reason to conclude that this Taker knows where we all live. I know none of you will panic, we've been there before, but be a little more careful than usual."

Lieutenant Daniels said, "Toni, it's your call, but I suggest we go home, get some of today washed off of us, and meet here tomorrow with a fresh resolve."

Toni was all for that, and readily agreed. As the task force began to leave, Toni pulled Adrian Keller to the side. Toni put her hand on Adrian's shoulder and said, "I know you haven't been here before. How do you feel about this possibility?"

"Me, I'm just a back room tech. I don't see this person coming after me," she said. Toni followed up, "I agree with you, however, would you like me to have a car roll past your home a couple of times each night, or do you have some friends you could stay with?"

"Oh, I'll be fine, just fine," Adrian said. "It's the out-front people, the cops who are at risk, not some clerk. I live alone, but I've got good locks on the doors and windows."

Toni nodded, "Well you're certainly a great deal more to us than a clerk," she added, "Let's hope you stay that way to The Taker. Anyway, we all have each other's mobile numbers. Don't hesitate to call whoever lives closest to where you are, for help, even if you think you hear a noise outside."

Seventeen

It was the morning of January 27th, the fifteenth day of the investigation. The squad's 8 o'clock meeting went nowhere, and Rosa Padilla was frustrated, as they all were. The SAPD was no closer to apprehending The Taker, than they were on day one. She was certain, however that there had to be a connection between the three non-gang victims, which they were not seeing. Yesterday, Sunday, had been thankfully peaceful on the "Taker" case, so the squad had time to recharge their personal batteries and delve headlong into the case, again.

She decided to make a second visit to Alamo Bank and Trust. It couldn't hurt. Making a third visit to the other companies whose employees had been murdered, would probably put them on the defensive...something she didn't want, especially if there was something there, beneath the surface.

After a phone call to Mr. Bloom's administrative assistant, requesting a second meeting, Rosa went back to her favorite diner, and had coffee and a pastry, to wait for the return call. She didn't have to wait long, as halfway through her coffee, her cell phone rang and she was granted a 30 minute audience, at 11 am. Great, now she just had to think of questions to ask, without being redundant.

Rosa pulled into the bank parking lot, early, and was in the 4th floor reception area at 10:55 sharp. After about 10 minutes, the receptionist said that Mr. Bloom was off the phone and would see her now. She was escorted into the huge corner office, and sat in the same high-back chair she had the first time she visited. Pleasantries were exchanged, with Rosa apologizing for the second intrusion. "I just want to get my facts 100% straight, and turn in my report," said Rosa. "Like I said before, anything I can do to help find Danny's killer, I'll do. He was a friend, and a valued employee."

Rosa pretended to look at her notes. She made little check marks beside some lines. Rosa asked, "I'm sure Danny banked here, but can you tell me if the first two victims had accounts at this bank?" Bloom appeared ready for this, "Like I said before, we can't discuss clients without a court order, but because of the personal nature of this crime, and my friendship with the ex-governor's family, I did some checking."

"What did you find?" Rosa asked. Bloom leaned toward her in a conspiratorial manner and whispered, "Neither of the victims had accounts here. No checking, savings, or CD's." Rosa replied, "Thanks, I know you didn't have to do that for us, but it helps eliminate a couple of things." She made a large checkmark on her notes, beside nothing pertinent to the bank, and looked up at the banker.

Just then, Bloom's cell phone rang, the ringtone being that of *Clair de Lune*, by Claude Debussy. "It's my wife," he said, "I have to take it, she's traveling to Houston, today."

Rosa got out of her chair to leave the room so he could speak with his wife, but Bloom said, "No, you stay here. I have a small conference room behind here," as he pointed to a door behind the desk. "I won't be a minute."

Rosa sat back in the chair. While waiting she started looking at the photos and civic awards on the walls. Bloom cutting the ribbon with the former mayor, Bloom with the governor, Bloom and pals on a hunting trip. Rosa's eyes locked on the hunting photo. There were 4 men, dressed

In camouflage outfits, shotguns over their shoulders. Rosa thought, I know these men. She got up for a closer look. Yes, she knew three of the men. Eugene Bloom, Allen Strudwick, Dave Williamson, and a fourth person she had not encountered. He was taller than the others, had a set of perfect teeth, and sandy hair, very handsome.

Rosa quickly took out her Blackberry cell phone, made sure the resolution was set to "best", stood to the side to eliminate glare from a flash, and quickly snapped two photos, of the hunting party displayed on the wall. They said they didn't know each other, Rosa thought. She sat down, just in time, as Bloom re-entered his office less than ten seconds later.

"Sorry for the interruption," he said, "Tammy wants to buy a Remington." Rosa looked at him with a puzzled expression. "Ah, yes, Frederic Remington crafted 22 bronze statues in the early 1900's. They are all collectors items, and are very expensive." He continued, "Of course, she said she wants to buy it for me, as a birthday gift."

Rosa commented, "What a nice thought. Well, I think I've taken up too much of your time. This completes my background check. You can tell the ex-governor, we will keep him updated." Rosa got up to leave, shook hands with Bloom, and said, "By the way, happy birthday."

On the way down the elevator she had but one thought, I've finally found a connection between the accountants, the lawyers, and the bank. Please, please, let the photos turn out to be identifiable. She drove back to SAPD with renewed vigor and interest. A few things were starting to come together. Once she got back to her desk, she decided to send the photos individually, in case of a mistake, to her own email.

There she could print them out. Her hands were shaking. Rosa had done this a thousand times. But, there was a big difference between sending your child's birthday or Christmas photos, and handling her first possible lead in a multiple murder case.

Rosa sat down behind her computer and opened *Outlook*. She located the first photo, attached it to a self addressed email and clicked send. Come on, come on, she begged. The message finally arrived. It was blank! There was a note at the bottom of the email which said, "The SAPD server has removed potentially hazardous attachments from this incoming message. Such attachments can contain dangerous viruses, and will not be accepted at this address."

"Oh shit," Rosa said under her breath. But all was not lost. Both photos were still on her Blackberry, she would just have to use her home computer to get the photos. Her home setup was mediocre, at best, but it would have to do. She grabbed her phone and purse and almost ran into Toni and Tom Granger, as they were coming in the door.

Toni asked, "Rosa, what's up? Have we had another killing?" Rosa hurriedly explained the situation to them, and why she was so urgent. Toni offered, "Lets go to my place, it's 10 minutes away, and I have a new computer with Windows 7, and a great photo enhancement program." Rosa quickly agreed. "Tom, you want to come?" Toni asked. He answered as expected, "I'm no good with this computer stuff. Just bring me the pictures, and lets see if we can catch this lunatic."

Toni and Rosa flew down the stairs, no elevator for these two, piled in Toni's unmarked car, and sped north up Highway 281 toward Toni's home.

Eleven minutes later, they pulled into Toni's driveway, Rosa had calmed down, a little. She knew that Toni was good with computers, and would handle the extraction of the photos from the Blackberry. They sat at the computer, and Toni carefully sent the photos to herself, again one at a time. It took about two minutes for the emails to arrive.

The attached photo was still in place on both. The first picture was about 90%. A little blurry, but Toni said that she could sharpen the pixels (whatever that meant to Rosa, it was good). The second photo was perfect. You could even count the teeth of the mystery man.

Toni made copies of the second shot on photo paper at a high resolution. She didn't want to make too many. This had to be a discreet investigation. If he was connected to the crimes, he could disappear, especially with the help of the others in the picture with him.

She made one copy of each for Rosa, Lt. Daniels, and herself. Then she cropped out the three known people, and made three copies of just the unknown man. It was their first break.

Eighteen

The daily 5 o'clock meeting was held with everyone arriving early. Toni could see the results of a Sunday off. A day without incident. A day of rest. The squad looked eager. She first stated that she and Tom had found no leads to a 45 semi-automatic, and that you could buy the Federal Hydra-Shok ammunition at over three dozen places, locally.

Adrian Keller reported no messages from The Taker, and limited chatter on related subjects. It had been a slow weekend, for the task force, but was filled with crimes by civilians. This was not Toni's responsibility at the time.

Billy stood, and related the lack of success he and Starr had had canvassing the bars and clubs. No one remembered seeing the victims.

Rosa had rehearsed her report. Per Toni's instructions, she recounted the return to the bank, her meeting with Mr. Bloom, the purchase of the Remington bronze, but nothing about the link she had found between the three companies who had employed the victims. That was something they needed to think about.

Toni excused the group, asking them to look into their areas of the investigation. Starr had not yet finished visiting all the gyms in the area, Billy was asked to check out the more suburban bars and clubs. Who was to say they had been abducted downtown? Tom knew what was going on with the photo, and would freelance, today.

As planned, Toni asked while everyone was leaving, "Rosa,

could you stay for just a minute? Rosa, of course, was expecting this. Toni had scheduled a meeting with Lt. Daniels, immediately following. They went across the hall to his door and knocked. He was on the phone, but looked up and waved them in.

He hung up, and asked, "What's up? Why the secrecy?" Toni explained. "We found, no that's not right, Rosa found, what we believe to be a link between the three companies who employed the victims," and she laid the photo of the hunters on Daniels' desk.

Daniels looked at the photo of the four men and smiled, "You think they're The Taker? That they committed the murders? These four guys?"

"No, not at all," Toni said. "What we think is, well you tell him, Rosa, you're the one who did all the interviews." Rosa began, "Boss, there's something not right here. Number one, I interviewed the HR people on the initial investigation. Then I decided to speak directly to the principals of the firm. They're the ones who know what's going on in their companies, not the underlings."

Rosa went on, "They were all warm and fuzzy, or as much as lawyers and CPAs can be, in the beginning. But when I asked about business from foreign accounts, all three firms stiffened, and showed lots of stress, almost identical behavior. I'm good at reading people."

"Then," she said, "there's the chart." Daniels interrupted, "Chart, what chart?" Rosa clarified. "When I went for the first interviews, with HR, I was given an organizational chart of the companies, you know, like who reports to who, etc. The accounting firm was very vague. It just showed who the clerks were, then the department heads, etc., same as the bank. But the lawyers chart showed that Paige Anders worked for a Peter Tan, in international law." Daniels asked, "What do you get from that?"

She explained, "On my second trip to the firms, I asked the principals for an organizational chart, mainly to stall for time. But this time, the lawyers at Cooper, Strudwick had changed their chart. It still had Anders on it, but she was reporting to someone in Real Estate named Blessing. I specifically asked before looking at the chart, and they said that she worked primarily for Blessing." Rosa concluded, "It just doesn't ring true, lieutenant. They're hiding something, I'm sure of that."

"You expect me to go to the captain with that?" he asked Toni. "No," she said, "then there's the photos," she said pointing again to the four hunters.

"And again, it doesn't prove anything," Toni admitted, "but during Rosa's second interview at the bank, the head man there, Bloom, had to leave his office for a phone call from his wife. Rosa spotted this photo on the wall, and took a picture of it," she said, handing a copy to the lieutenant. "What's this," he chided, "hunting out of season?"

Toni stood up and said, "Give us some credit, will you? It shows the principals of the Accounting, Legal, and Banking firms, together on a hunt, along with a man we haven't identified. It ties them together, even though they each told Rosa they don't know each other, except by reputation, and did no business together." Rosa chimed in, "And the answers to my questions were given by these two people, right here. Why did they lie about something so innocent?" she asked, pointing out Williamson and Strudwick in the photo.

Toni sat back down in her chair. "We're here to ask for your help and advice. We can't question loads of people about this guy. With his connections, if something is amiss, he'd be gone into the wind, we'd never find him."

Lieutenant Daniels looked up from the photo. "You may be on to something. I don't know what, or how it pertains to this case, but it's something." Toni admitted, "That makes three of us, Don."

The lieutenant shook his head, "I just don't know how to approach it," he said. "We've got to stay low profile, like you said, but we can't solve this puzzle without a great deal of help, or a lot of luck."

He thought out loud, and asked, "What do you think, I could go to Captain Bernardo, see if the boys in Austin can run it through their facial recognition scan. It's new, but it has all the driver's license photos in the database. We could get a hit?"

Toni answered, "Can he keep it quiet, from the other departments? And I mean real quiet," she repeated.

Daniels replied, "If anyone can, it would be Bernardo. All the cops, including State, have a lot of respect for him."

Toni asked another question, "Can we keep the Feds out? Too many damn leaks there."

Lieutenant Daniels said, "Yeah, we used to have to go to them with things like this. But the computer overhaul two years ago have given us as much capacity as anyone except Homeland Security, and this is certainly out of their jurisdiction."

He finalized his thinking, "Let me go to Bernardo, alone. No offense, but if I'm asking him for confidential assistance, he's going to want it confidential, in both directions, if you know what I mean. Just don't mention this to anyone."

With that, Don Daniels picked up his desk telephone, called Captain Bernardo's office and was given an immediate audience. He hung up and started to leave his office. "Not a word of this to anyone," he reminded Toni and Rosa.

Captain Bernardo was not in a particularly good mood over Lt. Daniels request. "I see this as a wild goose chase," he declared to the lieutenant. "But, since this is the only lead we have right now, I'll run with it. I'll probably be laughed out of a job, but let's just keep this to the four of us," he demanded.

Daniels agreed, and left the Captain's office only a little more shaken than when he entered, just five minutes ago. The Captain was taking this to the state, and that was all he was asking.

Nineteen

It was late Wednesday afternoon, and Starr Jones felt like she was at a dead end. How many bars and clubs had she been to in the past couple of weeks?

This investigation was going nowhere, and she didn't like it one little bit. It was Wednesday, 3 hours before the end of her shift, and the daily 5 o'clock meeting with another day of frustration heaped on her shoulders.

But, as the saying goes, "It's always darkest before the dawn." Her cell phone buzzed in vibration mode, and she answered, "Jones here." It was the SAPD switchboard, transferring a call from a citizen asking specifically for her. "Put 'em through," she replied, who could this be, she wondered?

She answered the transfer, "Investigator Jones here." The voice on the other end said, "Officer Jones, it's Darius." Starr thought for a minute, gave up, and asked, "Darius, who?" The man answered, "Darius White, from *The Blue Note* bar. My partner said you were in here showing a photo while I was on vacation, and I should call you when I got back. Well, I'm back. Would you like for me to look at that photo officer Jones?"

"Oh, Mr. White, I'm sorry I didn't remember. Of course I'd like you to see it. When would be convenient for you?" Darius replied, "Well, now is as good a time as any. We don't get busy till around eight or so, so I've got time." Starr quickly said, "I'll be there in thirty minutes, that OK?" Darius said it was, so she was off to downtown, and *The Blue Note*.

Fifteen minutes later, Starr pulled into the almost empty parking lot surrounding the jazz club. Darius was right, almost 3:30 pm and only two other cars visible.

She walked in, let her eyes adjust to the darkness, and the pervasive smell of tobacco smoke, and saw a large man standing with his back to the door, behind the bar. She walked up, as he saw her reflection in the bar mirror he turned. Starr asked "Are you Darius White?"

He gave a big grin which displayed a gold, star-shaped filling in one of his front teeth, "The one and only," he admitted. "And you must be officer Jones, my partner described you to a T, said I'd have no trouble spotting you."

Here we go again, Starr thought. Just what I need, another older man hitting on me. But Darius quickly changed the subject, before she had time to show her dismay. "Where's that picture you want me to look at?" he asked. Starr pulled three photos of the victims out of her file, and said, "We actually have three photos, two women and a man, for you to look at."

Darius examined each, carefully, holding them at arm's length to adjust for his aging vision. "Well, I never seen this guy here, looks a little light, to me." Starr withheld comment. "And this Anglo girl, never seen her either." He continued to review Angela Mendez' photo. "This girl, here, I definitely have seen her, not recently though, maybe late last year, December, I think. I remember her, 'cause we don't get many Mexicans in here, and she accidently was sitting under the mistletoe, which some of my patrons tried to take advantage of. She wouldn't have any of that though. She turned them down, flat." Starr questioned, "Are you sure?" Darius retorted, "Of course I'm sure. Wouldn't be much of a bartender if I wasn't observant, and she was with an Anglo chick too, but not that one there in your picture." Darius went on. "I thought they might have something going on, but it wasn't that, I can tell. They was here nursing a couple of cosmos for an hour, the Mexican girl, she went to the bathroom, and they left, together."

Starr pressed on, "Were either one of them drunk, or tipsy." Darius laughed, on one cosmo, I don't think so, but the, Mex...sorry, I guess the proper term is Hispanic," Starr nodded, she didn't want to get caught up in semantics, "she did stumble a little bit when she stepped out the door, didn't think much of it at the time, figured she missed the step."

Starr decided to take a chance, "Was there anyone else here that night, while they were here, who struck you as odd, or out of place?" Darius thought for a moment. "It was a busy night, but there was another Mex, I mean Hispanic man here, which is unusual for our crowd. But, he kept to himself, drank a couple of beers, and left before they did." Starr asked, "Would you recognize him if you saw him again, or can you describe him?"

Darius closed his eyes to remember, "No, he had on a large western hat, and was wearing jeans and a flannel shirt." This guy is good, thought Starr, but he had just identified about half the non-business types in the city, with that description. Then the bartender said something which could be important, "But he was huge. I don't mean fat, I mean about 6'5", 275 lbs, if he was an ounce. Wouldn't want to meet him in a dark alley." Star finished, "Mr. White, you've been a big help, call me if I can help you sometimes, in a professional way, I mean." Starr leaned over, kissed him on the cheek, and knew she had someone who could be a help in catching the murderer of three innocent people. Once outside, she called Toni on her cell phone. When she answered Starr exclaimed, "I've got a lead, a good lead." Toni responded, "That's good, because we have another body. You can tell me more about it when you get here."

Starr arrived at the scene in only about 20 minutes. It was just south of I-10 east, on FM (farm to market state road) 1604. The cause of death was the same, and the body had been dumped here, probably last night, the coroner estimated. Rigor mortis had definitely set in. It usually begins at three hours past death, then begins to cease at 12 hours post mortem.

At this early stage, this was all they had to work with. The body had been discovered by a motorist, it was at least 50 yards off the roadway, and wrapped in a yellow blanket. The coroner had measured the body temperature and examined the rigor at 2:45. He had placed the approximate time of death between midnight and 4 am, based on those two factors.

"So what do you have to tell me?" Toni asked, "and make it good, I need all the help I can get." Starr went through the interview with Darius White in great detail. "He's as credible a witness as I've had in any case. He even remembered what they were drinking, and who else was in the bar."

A really large man, huh, remembering Tom's observation of the Anders body, and now this one, being found so far from the road. She remembered thinking, "a really strong man" had to carry that dead weight, this one as well. Toni said, "Keep it till tomorrow. We'll discuss it at the 8 am meeting. I'm pretty sure the lieutenant will be there as well, especially after finding another victim today.

The deceased was a 28 year old white female, Susan Hershey, an architect who worked for Alexander & Archer, designers, here in San Antonio. Toni couldn't help but detect the same musty smell which she had encountered at the Lewis scene, on the clothing of the deceased. Probably a result of being beside a roadway for so long, she thought. Exhaust fumes.

Toni would make sure the relatives were notified, and send Rosa to see what, if anything, she could uncover at the design firm, tomorrow after the meeting. They probably weren't open at 8 am, anyway.

The lieutenant would call the firm and pave the way for Rosa's interviews, speaking to the owner or senior partner whenever possible. Unfortunately, he had plenty of practice.

Twenty

The next morning's meeting was abuzz with activity, conjecture, and gossip. Even Rosa and Adrian Keller were involved in the loud discussion, when Toni yelled, "Quiet...please people." They all settled down, just in time for the lieutenant, and Captain Bernardo to walk in, unannounced, and take seats at the table.

Toni had figured that Lieutenant Daniels would attend. Bernardo's presence meant that the pressure from above had just been turned up a notch or two.

Captain Bernardo spoke first, "I don't have to tell you that we are under enormous scrutiny from the public, the media, the chief, and the Mayor, not to mention our former Governor. I know you've all seen the headlines, and seen the news reports of The Taker. I'm here to report back to my superiors, any progress that has been made with the investigation in total. Can anyone share anything positive with me, which would help me keep the wolves away from my door?"

Toni acted proactively, as was her nature with authority figures. "Yesterday," Toni answered, "we found a solid witness who saw the Mendez woman, and the person she was with, on the night of her murder." She added, "We're trying to piece together a timeline which fits her murder, then go to other places and see if we can recreate a similar scenario, there."

Following up, she explained their plan of action, "It may be easier to track the activities of Dan Lewis, not because he was gay, but because he was very particular about the places where he went, and who he was seen with. We have a list of about a dozen places he frequented. We'll start there, first."

"Well, that's more than I expected," Bernardo said. This will help show progress in the case. Any linkage to the most recent victim and the others, or is that asking too much?" the captain questioned.

Toni answered, "Rosa is going out to her firm at 10:30 this morning. She's the same one who interviewed the other companies. She'll know if there's a link."

"OK," said Bernardo, "but keep me informed, immediately, if possible," and he rose to leave the meeting. Daniels leaned over to Toni and whispered, "No hits on the photo, either. The guy must not have a Texas driver's license."

Toni tried not to look disheartened, but she was. That photo could have cleared up a lot of things.

"Alright folks, here's what Starr found out," Toni said, and she let Starr have her time in the spotlight describing her interview at *The Blue Note*, in great detail, right down to the huge man who was present, at least for part of the time, and the slight stumble by Mendez when the two women were leaving the bar.

"It's back on detail, Starr and Billy, see if any of the clubs remember a huge man in a cowboy hat and flannel shirt. Most of these guys don't change their wardrobes at the whim of fashion. Rosa's going out to where Hershey worked, Tom and I will revisit the scene where the body was found. "If you find anything special, call me at once." Toni concluded.

Toni asked, even though she knew the answer, "Adrian, any

messages?" Adrian turned on the slide projector. "It came in at 7 am," she said.

The Hits just Keep on Coming...Don't They?

Have You Gotten My Message Yet?

The Gangs, People, The Gangs

You Could stop This Madness Now

The Next Message Will Be in the Press

The Taker

The group was angry. Another taunt. Another snipe directed at them. Toni said, "We just have to work smarter...we're getting closer, I can feel it."

Then she said "Rosa, stay behind for a minute." Once the group was gone, Toni told Rosa that the photo came up a big zero, with the State boys. "Doesn't mean it's not a key to the case," Toni said, "It means that he just doesn't have a Texas driver's license." Now, go see what the architects have to say for themselves."

Rosa's appointment was with Thomas Alexander, founder and majority owner of the firm. Early that morning she had run the credit check and NCIC report on the victim, which came back just as the others. Very little debt, no arrests, etc., etc. Meeting with Alexander, he too, extolled the virtues of his former employee. Susan Hershey had been an employee there in the CAD department since she graduated with her engineering degree from Texas A&M, six years ago. Like the other victims, she had excellent performance evaluations during her tenure, was highly respected in her field, and no one could think of any reasons that someone would harm her. Rosa spent the next three hours, speaking with human resources and Susan's co-workers. No one knew anything of a possible motive, she dated, but never with people at the firm, and never very seriously, as far as they knew. Everyone was shocked, and had a "that could have been me" feeling of dread.

As planned, Rosa stopped by Mr. Alexander's office on the way out to thank him. "I forgot one question, I hope you don't mind." He responded, "Not at all, anything I can do to help find whoever did this horrible thing, I'm glad to help."

" Thanks," Rosa said, "I knew you'd feel that way. I was just wondering about your business. Do you do mostly local business, or is some of it international?"

Alexander didn't flinch. "We've never done any international design business, wish we did. We have done a little out of state, but 95% is within sixty miles of San Antonio, why do you ask?" Rosa replied, "Just curious, trying to see how different businesses work, that's all. Well, I really appreciate your help. It seems that everyone here was really fond of Susan," Rosa said. "Now I'll get out of your way, and let you get back to your busy schedule."

Alexander added, "Please call me if you have anything you want to know." Rosa waved, "You call me if you think of something I missed. It won't bother me at all."

She couldn't see any international connection there. Alexander hadn't missed a beat when the question had been raised concerning the source of his business. Rosa had been in too many interrogations and questionings to be easily fooled. It appeared the design firm was outside the loop. After all, they weren't in the hunting photo, for all the good that meant. Well it was 3 o'clock, and with all the new activity, Toni had decided to pass up the 5 pm meeting.

It was a good time for Rosa to get some extra time with her two teenagers. This was a difficult time for young girls, turning into women. With no father, and a mother who obsessed over murderers and gang crimes, Rosa was lucky to have such well adjusted kids. They both made the honor roll every semester.

Rosa had told them right after their father had been killed in Iraq, that he had died to protect their freedom. The best way to honor his memory, was to make good grades, and hope for college scholarship help. With a degree, she had told them often, they could be anything they wanted to be in this country.

Maria, and Anna were model children, partly out of respect for their father, and mostly because Maria, who was 16 now, had assumed the role of guiding Anna through tough times when their mom couldn't be there.

The girls had been home from St. Mary's school for only about 30 minutes when Rosa surprised them with an early arrival from work. "Who's for ice cream?" Rosa asked, knowing the excited answer... "meeeeee," they said in stereo, especially the thirteen year old, Anna, who wasn't into watching her figure, yet.

They drove the half mile to Baskin Robbins, got a table and studied the menu of flavors, even they probably knew its' contents as well as their ABCs. Rosa decided to let Maria cook for the evening. It was good practice, and Rosa got to sit back and have her one glass of wine she allowed herself each evening.

Both of her parents had been alcoholics, and she had sworn to herself that she would never fall into that trap of dependency, which they did. She wanted her girls to grow up without the fighting, the hangovers, and the verbal abuse she had. And Rosa thought, just like an alcoholic did, one day at a time, so far, so good. She knew she had the alcoholic gene.

Toni and Tom were at the scene where the body of Susan Hershey was found. Again they covered the same ground that the forensics team had, just from a detective's perspective. Tom observed, "Just like the Anders body, would have taken a lot of strength to get that body all that way from the highway."

They didn't find anything which the crime scene techs had missed, they rarely did. And since they knew the woman was killed somewhere else, and her body dumped here, there wasn't much else they could do there.

Toni decided it was time to tell Tom about the hunting group photo which Rosa had taken at the bank, and how Captain Bernardo had run it through the State's facial recognition software and come up empty. She assured him, "We weren't trying to keep it a secret, it's just that it could have been something. It turned out to be a dead end, so we dropped it."

Tom thought about this for a while. He observed, "I've been hunting for 30 years. I've never gone on a trip with strangers. Now maybe that's just me, and they way I am, but I don't think so. I'd say the odds are they were pretty good friends. The banker, the accountant, the lawyer, and whoever this mystery man is, are probably more than just acquaintances." He added, "A person can't trust new people with guns, especially since you said they were shotguns, they were quail or turkey hunting. Lots of danger there."

He explained, "Birds fly across your field of vision, and guns follow their flight. It's easy to get so locked in on a moving target that you forget that the other hunters are locked in as well. You've got to call your shot, especially with quail. No ma'm, I'd say they knew each other real well."

This gave Toni some hope. Maybe something would come out of it. But, how to do it? She could confront one of the three known men in the photo, and they could say he was their guide, or something similar. How could she tie them together.

Toni had a thought. "Tom, my friend Rhonda is coming over tomorrow night. We have dinner a couple of times a month. It's her turn, but her kitchen is being redone. How'd you like to come join us?"

Tom turned red, Toni had never seen this side of him. "Oh, I'd just be in the way," he said. "An old guy like me, and you girls are friends, I don't know. "I insist," said Toni. "When's the last time you had a home cooked meal?

"It's been a while," he answered. "That does it," said Toni, "and bring two bottles of red wine, we're having pasta, be there at 7, you know the way."

Twenty One

The 8 am meeting Friday morning went pretty much the way the other meetings had gone. The main difference today, was that Susan Hershey's name had been added to the list of victims on the white board.

Rosa was first. Without boring you, let me just say that this young woman was as vanilla as the previous victims, with the exception of the gang leader, Carlos Ruiz.

No bad debt, no husband or lover that we know of, no arrest record, no IRS investigation or liens. She rented a home just on the west side of the city, near Ingram Mall, graduated with honors six years ago from Texas A&M, and drove a 5-year old Volvo. We should all have kids who grow up like her, just not dead.

Starr and Billy had struck out at the bars and clubs. They knew most of the bartenders in town by this time. Most wanted to help, but could not identify the most recent victim.

Adrian reported that there were no new messages, but none had been expected.

Toni told the group that the scene where the body had been found had been searched by Tom and her for over two hours, with no progress. It had, however, demonstrated that an extremely strong person, or two people had been necessary to move the dead weight of Susan Hershey, 162 feet off the road. The large man who had been observed at *The Blue Note*, was back in the conversation, but on purely circumstantial findings. You couldn't put out an APB on large men, you just had to keep your eyes open. The task force had factored this into the search and questioning parameters after Rosa had told them of his presence at the last known sighting of Angela Mendez.

Toni made another command decision. "Providing nothing else turns up today, no bodies and no serious clues, I want everyone off the clock and on the way home by 2 o'clock. This team has been going at this case non-stop, you've all worked 70-hour weeks, including several weekends, and we need to have a life outside the department."

Toni finished with, "Any objections?" There were none, in fact, there was a large exhale, with heads nodding in the group. They all left the 7th floor conference room, and went their separate ways. They all seemed relieved to be getting even a couple of extra hours off-duty.

Starr called her boyfriend, Clarence, (everyone called him CJ, it was a lot cooler than Clarence Jefferson) and made an early evening date. The Spurs were playing the Houston Rockets, so it would be an NBA game and a late dinner somewhere down on the River Walk. She had a favorite steak house she loved and would lobby for that. Then she thought, to hell with lobby, she called for 9:30 reservations, allowing enough time for the game to finish.

Rosa was thrilled to have extra time at home with her girls for the second day in a row. She could taste the ice cream already. She decided that today being Friday, the family could have a "girls night at home", and save any school work until the weekend.

Adrian Keller was beat, but went back to IT, to scan for incoming emails, and sit her watch at the screens, even though she had been transferred to the task force until the case was closed.

Billy called Rita Estrada. He would meet her downtown just after her newscast on Channel 13, at 5 pm. A side benefit to Billy's investigation had been his discovery of a couple of new clubs he wanted to take Rita to. He loved showing her off. She was something of a celebrity, herself.

Tom would use the extra time deciding what to wear over to Toni's house for dinner tonight. He knew it wasn't a "date." after all, her friend Rhonda was coming over as well. But, he hadn't been in the presence of a woman in a non-business atmosphere for years. He wanted to make a good impression.

Toni would go shopping for fresh made pasta at a little Italian gourmet shop she had discovered. She was planning on serving sausages (turkey, not pork, which was more heart healthy) and had phoned Rhonda asking her to bring enough Caesar salad ingredients for three people, with no anchovies. She told Rhonda Tom's background, to avoid any faux pas references to marriages or ex-wives, and Rhonda was enthusiastic about the upcoming dinner.

Twenty Two

Tom Granger rang the doorbell at exactly 7 pm, which is what Toni expected. He was a most efficient and punctual person by habit. For meetings, or a beer after work at one of the bars the cops frequented, he was the first to get there, and usually the first to leave, as well.

"I hope Chianti is OK," Tom asked. "You said we were having pasta," as he handed Toni two bottles wrapped in special gift bags.

"Oh, this is perfect," Toni said. That's something else about you I didn't know about. You know your wines."

"Not exactly," Tom admitted. "It was a recommendation from the man at the wine shop," he said sheepishly.

"Another attribute." Toni bragged, "Most men are afraid to ask for help, especially with wine or driving directions." They both got a laugh out of that truism.

"Well," Toni looked around, "I'm not through picking up the place yet. I still have my computer station full of paperwork and cop stuff, plus the occasional invoice from someone. Give me two minutes, and the clutter will be hidden." Tom thought, looks clean to me, but he made no comment. Toni powered off her computer, and began picking up her mess, stacking everything on the bottom shelf of an end table in the living room.

"You still have that hunting photo?" Tom asked. "Yes, Toni said, let me see, it's here in the stack. Voila," she said, pulling it out of the jumble of paperwork, "here it is." Toni commented, handing the photo to Granger. Tom studied the shot for a moment and asserted, "Yep, it was quail they were after. Small gauge shotguns so as not to blow all the meat off the bones."

Toni added, "Now if we could find this face, pointing to the mystery man in the picture, in the police database, and I.D. him, we'd have another piece of the puzzle. He doesn't have a Texas license, but I can't send this picture to all the surrounding states, without getting the Feds involved."

"I've never seen any of them before," Tom said, "but that's nothing new. All I can say is that they were handling their guns properly, and it wasn't their first hunt." He put the photo back beside the computer, as he thought he might study it again before he left. You never know what another look can turn up, he thought.

About then, Rhonda knocked and walked in the front door, like it was her own home. That's the kind of relationship she and Toni enjoyed. Toni would say, "Mi casa es su casa," all the time, and it went both ways for them.

Toni made the introductions and helped Rhonda with her Caesar salad ingredients. She put a pot of water on the gas stove to boil for the linguini, and said, "Tom, why don't you open one of those bottles. Don't know about you, but Rhonda and I cook better while we're having wine."

She slid a corkscrew across the granite countertop, which Tom scooped up, deftly, in his left hand. "Just like a ground ball to shortstop," Tom said. "Yeah, I played a little ball as a kid. Not good enough to make the majors, but not too bad, either."

He opened the first bottle, smelled the cork like he knew what he was doing, and poured a half glass each, into the three that Rhonda handed him. "Salud," Toni said as they clinked their glasses together.

The sauce smelled wonderful, the sausage was coming along, and Rhonda was almost finished with the salad.

Tom wandered over to the computer station, and started studying the hunters' photo again. He wasn't cooking, so he tried to look busy with something.

Rhonda walked over to where Tom was standing, looked over his shoulder. She asked, "Who're these three guys with Brad Perry? Looks like a hunting trip to me."

Toni and Tom immediately locked eyes. Toni turned the flame on the stove down, and walked over. "Which one," asked Toni. "The cute one, of course. The one with the sandy hair," Rhonda explained, pointing at the mystery man.

"And, you know this man, how?" asked Toni. "Oh, he's the developer of the 'Heart of Texas' mega mall, opening this fall. You have to go through him, before you can enter lease negotiations. He says they want the right mix of quality stores and high-end restaurants."

Rhonda continued, "The venture is called Tex-Mex Retail Ltd. I don't know where they get the 'Mex' part, he's from Arizona, Phoenix, I think. He just laughed when I asked him about it, why?"

Toni looked at Tom, who barely shook his head, when Rhonda wasn't looking. Toni said, casually, "We just had discussions with a couple of the other guys, and wondered who he was, no big deal. Let me get back to the sauce, I don't want to burn it." Tom changed he subject, "Rhonda, how is the retail business these days?" he asked. She answered, not bad in my little niche. People who wear small sizes can't find designer clothes easily, so they'll pay to keep from going to New York or L.A." she said. "But enough about business, I'm starved," Rhonda exclaimed. "Me too," added Tom.

The meal was wonderful, as everyone dug in. Tom and Toni were preoccupied in thought, but kept the banter going, throughout dinner.

Toni had even bought some canoli at the pastry shop for desert, along with cappuccino. Tom looked up at the two women and said, "This is the finest dinner I've had in years; and the best company as well."

The wine was long gone, the dessert finished and everyone pushed back from their chair. Rhonda excused herself from the table to powder her nose.

"Got anything planned for Saturday, Tom?" Toni asked. Tom replied, "I was thinking about taking a little drive up I-35, get some fresh air," he replied.

"Pick me up at 10," Toni said. "We may be on to something, can't hurt to look around."

Tom agreed, "And I know a great little German lunch place in New Braunfels, right nearby, so it won't be a total waste of our time."

Toni replied, "I have a hunch about this. You mind if I ask Rosa to tag along? I know she values her time with her kids, but she's the one who got us started down this track."

Tom laughed, "Tell her to bring 'em. They just might like an authentic German lunch. Probably haven't had Sauerkraut in their lives." Toni laughed, "Neither have I, and we have a famous German Deli, *Schilo's*, right downtown. Tom warned, but, they won't all fit in my truck, so we'll have to use your cruiser, if that's OK." Toni said, "Sure, police business, right?"

Rhonda returned from the ladies room, and after she and Tom helped Toni clean up the kitchen, they all said their goodnights. The three of them had hit it off, and combined with the bonus discovery, had been a most enjoyable time.

As soon as the front door was closed, Toni was on the telephone with an excited Rosa Padilla.

Twenty Three

The next morning Tom pulled up in front of Toni's house at 9:55. Rosa's car was already there. He walked up and rang the bell, then entered when Toni opened the door.

Tom had never met Rosa's daughters, but there they were, properly seated on the couch, sitting quietly. The only sign of anticipation were the huge smiles the girls were wearing.

Rosa stood and made the introductions. Maria stood and extended her hand, "So pleased to meet you," she said, and sat back on the couch. Anna was just as polite, saying, "My pleasure," before retreating to her former spot. They were both wearing jeans, clean and pressed.

Tom was somewhat taken aback, taking his Stetson hat off, and bowing slightly, to the girls. He wondered, were kids really like this? Knowing the answer, he mentally gave Rosa credit for the girls exemplary behavior.

"Well young ladies, I understand you're going to take a little drive up to New Braunfels with us, is that right?" The girls replied simultaneously, "Yes sir."

Tom announced, Then let's get on our way, there's wiener schnitzel, potato pancakes, and bratwurst, ready to be eaten. The five of them left the house and began to pile into Toni's Crown Victoria, unmarked cruiser. Unmarked, but easily identifiable as a police vehicle, none the less.

The girls jumped in the back, and Tom put up his hand to Rosa. "Would you mind if I sat in the back with your daughters?" he asked. You could have toppled both Rosa and Toni, with a feather. But, Tom knew what he was doing. He knew their father had been killed in Iraq. It was clear, they were starved for some fatherly attention. The girls were saying, "Please, Mom, let him sit with us."

"Are you sure?" asked Rosa. "It would be my pleasure," Tom answered back. Rosa looked at Toni who was beaming, and Rosa got in the passenger side with Toni driving.

Saturday morning traffic was light on the outer loop I-410. They passed complexes of office buildings whose parking lots were vacant. Then they passed North Star Mall, on the right side of the highway. It's parking lot was definitely not vacant. It would be a big shopping day there.

As they were driving, Tom would point out attractions and points of interest to the girls. Tom being a life-long resident of San Antonio, had it's benefits in his "tour guide" role.

Eventually they got to the I-35 North exit, and Tom pointed out Universal City, which was not a theme park, but a community which was the gateway to Randolph Air Force Base. He continued to answer their questions, mainly about the many small towns, and how San Antonio had changed during his lifetime. "You wouldn't believe it," he started, and went into the historical perspective on the growth and expansion of the city.

Tom then discussed the little strip of I-35 they would be entering into. It was called the Texas hill country, about halfway between San Antonio and Austin. New Braunfels, and a couple of smaller towns were settled by German migrants beginning in 1845. They continued to have Oktoberfest, and many German traditions, even today. The atmosphere in this small town would be something the girls had never been exposed to. Tom promised them, "You're in for a treat." The girls were rapt with attention, and also in anticipation of seeing something new in their lives. German culture would be quite a difference for them.

Toni and Rosa had been listening, as well. Rosa whispered to Toni, "I've never seen them take to someone as quickly as this." Toni nodded, and the women were proud of the extra attention Tom was giving the girls. Maria and Anna hung on every word Tom spoke.

There was a little period of quiet for a couple of minutes, giving Rosa a chance to talk to the girls. She turned her body toward the back seat so she could look at her daughters. "Are you two behaving back there? You're not badgering Mr. Granger, are you?"

Tom answered for them, "We're having a great time back here. I was about to ask the girls about their school, but, hey, it's a holiday for them. Why talk about school until we have to on Monday."

"Well, just don't let them be constant chatterboxes," Rosa said. "There's always a need for some quiet time in the car, especially for people not used to constant questioning."

Tom retorted, "I've been questioning for almost twenty five years now. I don't mind being on the other end for girls as bright and well behaved as these two. We're fine," he concluded.

Toni could see the signs just beginning. "Only 5 miles to the Heart of Texas Mall. The largest oasis in Texas. Shopping, dining, and entertainment for the entire family. Opening Fall This Year. In a few minutes Toni spotted the new exit which had been created expressly for this destination. The governor had said that only one year's worth of sales tax receipts would pay for the entire projected highway exit costs.

Toni took the exit and entered the construction site, which was mainly idle for the weekend. They still had six months to finish the project. She saw a large sign at the edge of where the parking lot and garage would be. They were stunned:

The Heart of Texas Mall

Developed by Tex-Mex Retail Ltd.

Alexander & Archer Design Engineers

Funded by Alamo Bank & Trust

**For Leasing Information Contact Brad Perry @ 800-555-3488,
or inquire locally, with Allen Strudwick @ 210-473-2133**

It was all there, as plain as the nose on your face. The developer, the design group, the bank, and the attorney, Allen Strudwick. No, the CPA firm wasn't listed, but why would they be? Rosa's face darkened as if a cloud had passed between she and the sun. But, it wasn't the lighting. She had been lied to, and there was nothing she hated more, than to be treated as a fool. Rosa snapped off a couple of photos showing the sign, and returned to a smiling, motherly façade, immediately.

"Who's for touring New Braunfels, and having a hearty German lunch?" Rosa asked. "We are, we are," the girls answered enthusiastically.

"Well then what's keeping us here?" Toni asked. There won't be shopping here for months, let's go." And with that, Toni pulled out of the construction area, found the I-35 north ramp, and headed toward their next destination.

I-35 runs right past the city of New Braunfels. Only fifteen more minutes and Tom said "Take the next exit, it's where most of the traditional shopping is, and is close to my favorite restaurant, here." They exited, found some city parking, and curiously ended up on West San Antonio Street, location of the Downtown Antique Mall. They all got out of the cruiser and had a big stretch. They had only been in the car a little more than an hour, but the last few minutes seemed much longer.

Tom said, "The Mall starts right her on the next corner. They have dozens of shops of all kinds and cultures."

Rosa had a diversion planned. "Girls, we need to find a public restroom, so we won't have to worry about that later, while we're shopping." Tom pointed out the international sign for the public facilities and they all walked toward it.

Rosa said, "You two girls go first, and we'll go after you're done." Maria and Anna dutifully walked the remaining twenty feet or so to the entrance. Once they were inside, Rosa's rage surfaced, "Those lying bastards, I'm going back and shove a photo of that sign up their ass!" she exclaimed. "What do they think, that I'm a stupid Mexican who can't investigate a murder. And these are murders surrounded by lies. Just wait till Monday, then we'll see."

Toni and Tom each grabbed an elbow of Rosa's. Toni whispered, "Don't take it personally. You said yourself, murders wrapped in lies. Rosa look at the big picture. If we're going after a conspiracy theme here, we need a lot more than we've got."

Rosa looked to Tom for support, but he agreed, "These boys are hard wired, well connected. You go after them now, they'll cover their tracks so fast we'll all be doing school crossings, if we still have jobs."

"We've got to play this smart, dig deeper, but keep it even quieter than before. Us three are the only ones who have connected a few dots. I'm bettin' there are a lot more dots out there, bigger ones, too."

Just then the girls came out of the facilities, and the 3 cops were all smiles again. Tom offered to Toni and Rosa, "OK ladies, your turn, I'll go last." The women went inside and Tom was sure the discussion was continuing, but the three of them couldn't hear a word of it out here.

After an unusually long time, the women exited, all smiles again. Tom said, "See that shop over across the street? The one named "Marx, Saddle and Tack"? I'll use the facilities here, and catch up with you in that store."

The women were fine with that, and Tom entered the other

side of the restroom building. As he came out, he was wondering what would possibly be the best way to handle the information they had stumbled upon. Thank God for Rhonda, and her retail shops, he thought to himself.

He entered the shop and saw his four companions. Toni and Rosa were watching the girls fascination with the riding equipment. The store clerk was patiently explaining the function of the bit, the stirrups, the saddle horn, etc. and the girls were entranced.

They gravitated to the boots, but there were none small enough for them. Even at 16, Maria was still wearing children's sizes. Tom figured that would change in a year or two.

Then they were trying on hats. Black hats, straw hats, hats of all types. They both seemed to like the hats styled after Tom's beige Stetson. Finally, Rosa interrupted, with "There are lots more shops to see, ladies, we should be moving on." And, with that they obediently put down what was in their hands and headed toward the door, followed by the adults. "Just a minute," Tom said when they were all outside. He stuck his head back in the shop said something to the clerk, and caught up.

"What was that about?" asked Toni. "Wanted to find out if he carried Lucchese boots, they're my favorite brand. He said they didn't, but could order them," Tom explained. "Don't know about you, but I usually have to try on about six pair, to find a good fit, so I hate to order them."

Toni agreed, "Same way it is for me," she said. "Even the brands I love, all the styles fit my foot a little differently."

With that, the group was off to see antique stores, the girls were amazed at cuckoo clocks, and their workings, as well as some of the ornate desks, primarily reproductions, and the other office fixtures like chairs, and lamps.

Eventually it was lunch time, and as promised, Tom had a special treat in store for the group. Just down the street and around a corner was the famous *Friesenhaus Llc*, purveyor of all good German food.

The group entered and it was typical Rausthause style, some tables, but mostly group seating at picnic style tables with built in bench seats. They located an open picnic table, and Tom asked if they could have it, the waiter instantly agreed. Tom sat on one side, flanked by the girls, Toni and Rosa on the other.

As the waiter approached with menu's, Tom looked at the waiter and said "Wie gehts, herr ober. Haben sie ein speisekarte in Englisch?" Toni's jaw dropped six inches. So did the others at the table. He speaks German?

"Gehts gut, Naturlich." he answered, flipping the menu's over to show the English translation on the back.

Tom spoke to the waiter again, "Funf wasser, bitte, und dann bestellen wir. Ich spreke ein wenig Deutsch. So we will order in English," he said without missing a beat.

Rosa asked, "How did you learn German?" Tom shrugged it off, "I just know a little. Uncle Sam had me over there for a couple of years, and I made it a point to learn their language, thought it was respectful. Especially since I was an MP. It really gets people to trust you, if you show some courtesy."

The waiter returned with five glasses for water, and asked Tom if they were ready to order. Tom looked around the table at four blank faces. It looked like the decisions were his, the others being completely unfamiliar with German cooking.

"Would you ladies like me to decide for you?" he asked, and four heads nodded in unison. "OK then, for appetizer we'll all have the sausage sampler, German potatoes, and bread. For our main course the young ladies will share a Weiner Schnitzel with rosti, the ladies across from me, and I, will have jaegerschnitzel (pork, not veal as in Weiner schnitzel) with cream sauce, and rosti. He looked at Toni and Rosa, wine or beer? "None for me, I'm driving, said Toni." Rosa was curious, "I've never had a German wine before."

Tom asked, "white or red, sweet or dry?" Rosa replied, "White and dry." Tom looked at the waiter and said "Weiss und trocken, und ein bier fir mish, bitte."

Tom explained, "In Germany, this is the main meal of the day, but don't try to finish if you get full. The strudel here is great, so is the cheesecake."

The sausage sampler arrived, along with warm German bread, butter and a nice homemade sauce with horse radish. Everyone dug in. Rosa approved of her wine, the selection made by Tom.

The main courses were grand. Tom was smart to let Maria and Anna share a meal, it was enough for three people. None of the adults could finish, and heeded Tom's advice not to stuff themselves. He ordered apple strudel for the table, with vanilla ice cream on top, coffee for the adults, tea for the girls. It literally melted in their mouths.

The check came, and Toni insisted that the department pay for the meal. Tom objected. "If we're going to keep this between us, we might as well begin now. I think we should split it three ways, that way it's still between us. We were never together, it was just an ordinary weekend day." Rosa agreed, but wanted to pay more since she had the girls. "No way," said Toni, "the bill is only $60, you can leave the tip." It was settled.

Everyone was stuffed, despite the earlier warning, and they stumbled out of the restaurant.

The girls were already yawning, as they walked back to the car. "Last chance for the bathroom," Rosa said, and the four women went in one side, and Tom the other. I guess the four of them took longer than Tom, because when they came out, Tom was standing on the street corner with two small boxes strung together.

"What's that," asked Toni. "Just a little western remembrance of the trip for the girls," Tom said, and he handed the boxes to the squealing girls. "You can't do that," Rosa said. "I just did," Tom replied, "and the store doesn't accept returns."

Maria and Anna ripped open their boxes and put their beige western hats on for the trip home. Toni kept thinking, who is this man?

Rosa tried to scold Tom, but he wasn't buying into it. "Today's the best time I've had in years. And a big part of the reason, is these two," he said pointing at the girls. "What else can I spend my money on that gives me so much satisfaction? Nothing, that's what. Forty three, going on forty four years old, I felt young again for the first time in years. And you know the best part, Rosa, they're great young women. You've brought them up the right way. They're respectful, polite, and behave the way you taught them to. Trump that!"

Well, she couldn't, and they walked to the cruiser for the trip home. After about fifteen minutes, the girls had nodded off. Toni looked back and made a suggestion. "I think we should keep this among us, until we develop a strategy, for proceeding. I think we have a tiger by the tail. This investigation, inside another investigation, will either make us, or break us."

Rosa said, "I've been thinking. I have a very good girlfriend. She's the best computer hacker I've ever heard of. If she can't tie this together, it doesn't exist. I'll call her tomorrow." Toni asked, "You can trust her?" Rosa asserted, "With my life."

"That's good," Toni said in return, "because you may be."

Twenty Four

Toni had her usual Monday morning meeting with the crew. "Now we have to get lucky, she said. And the best way to create a break in the case involves old-fashioned police work. Back to the streets, asking and repeating the same questions." Toni heard the usual groans from the group, but that was to be expected.

After the meeting, Rosa pulled Toni aside. "I spoke to my hacker friend, Marta, yesterday. This morning I dropped off a list of everything we knew about the Heart of Texas project, and who the players are. She knows how to get information from everyone connected to the web...and everyone is connected to the web."

Rosa continued, "She said she'll have answers by the end of the week. I had to promise her a reward if anything comes out of this, so she's working for us, for free, if she doesn't produce results."

"And Tom," Rosa said turning to him, "I want to thank you for your time with the girls Saturday. They wore their new hats all day Sunday, except for going to Mass."

"Think nothing of it," Tom said, "I had a great time with them. They're great girls, and I don't even like kids," he admitted.

The three cops returned to the business at hand, which was to see how these companies were linked. The murder victims worked there, and they were all involved with the mall, but there must be more to it than met the eye.

Toni asserted, "All we can do in the mean time is the usual police work, and hope Marta comes up with something. However, it's vital that no one know what we might suspect. At this moment the interaction of these companies is not a crime, and we see no linkage to The Taker case. It's purely speculation."

Tom, who had also held back from leaving, agreed. "This has to be our strategy, but just for now. We know that people are lying, they're trying to hide something. Maybe something big."

He turned to Rosa and asked, "Do you think any of the bosses you spoke with were being honest?" She thought about it a minute and replied, "Maybe the design people, Alexander and Archer. He didn't have any reaction to the international business question, he just said they did mainly local business, which the new mall definitely is."

"The others though, were lying through their teeth, the photo shows that." They were hiding their knowledge of knowing each other, and doing business together. Why?"

No one had the answer to that. Right now was just sit and wait. Something the three of them definitely didn't like doing. The day dragged on, with the 5 pm meting yielding nothing of interest.

That night at 8:30, Toni's cell phone came to life with the task force ringtone. She was able to get to it on the second ring. Starr was on the other line, and was frantic. "The big man is following me, I'm sure of it," Starr whispered into the phone. "Where are you, I mean exactly?" Toni asked. "I'm at the corner of Commerce and Colorado, about 100 yards from Alejandro's Restaurant." Toni said "Go in there and sit at the bar. I'll be there in 15 minutes." Starr protested, No, I'll lose him, he'll go away. I've seen him tailing me, I want to get him out in the open," she said.

Toni barked, "Into the bar, that's an order. Do it!" Toni jumped into the cruiser. Calling dispatch she said, "10-48, Officer needs assistance, stalked by man who is multiple murder suspect. Suspect is extremely large Hispanic male, who should be considered armed and dangerous. Officer on the scene in Alejandro's Bar, proceed with caution. Seal off 4 block radius."

By the time she got to the scene, 3 squad cars were present, with four more participating in the 16 block search area. Starr was outside the restaurant with Billy and Tom. She had called both within minutes of Starr's call. They lived closer than Toni to the location.

"We blew it," Starr said, angrily. "I should have baited him into an alley, and taken him down."

Toni was about to blast her, but Billy beat her to the punch. "The guy has been described as 6'5", 275 pounds and we know he owns a 45 caliber semi-automatic. That's not anything any of us should attempt, alone, probably not even any two of us should try. Where's your head, girl? You were lucky." "I agree," said Tom. "That's just what he was hoping for. Another victim…this time a cop. A real trophy for his wall."

The patrol sergeant reported in that no persons resembling the suspect had been encountered, but he put out a BOLO with the description. He also doubled the squad cars on duty in the downtown area for tonight. The man was likely holed up somewhere, but if he showed his face, he would be stopped and questioned. Toni told the group that they would review their ongoing strategy in situations such as this at tomorrow morning's meeting, but admonished Starr, and everyone else involved, to go home for the evening.

Toni drove home, in an inevitable low mood after seemingly coming so close. She pulled up and parked in the driveway. As she approached her door, she saw that it had been kicked in, actually shattered. She got back in the cruiser and called Tom, he only lived two miles away. He was there in less than 5 minutes, along with two squad cars, and a crime scene van.
After a thorough search of the house, it was empty. In fact, the forensic people doubted that whoever kicked in the door had actually entered the house.

"He just wanted you to know that he knew where you lived," Tom said. "He baited us downtown and doubled back to do this." That was of little comfort to Toni. She made three phone calls on her cell. One to a 24-hour contractor she had used for civilian victims in the past. He would board up the front door and replace all the exterior doors with steel doors and frames, tomorrow.

She called a locksmith to add dead bolt and other tamper-resistant locks to the doors, and then she called Rhonda, to see if she and Buster could stay with her a couple of nights, which was fine with her. "Stay as long as you want," her friend offered. After the emotion had subsided, for the second time tonight, she thanked Tom, and told him she could handle it from here.

A squad car stayed long enough for her to pack the essentials she would need for a couple of days, and promised to stay until the contractor got there. Toni saw him pulling up just then, and sent the squad car on his way. Toni reiterated what she wanted, gave the man her cell number for any problems, and left, driving a circuitous route to Rhonda's home.

Once she was certain that she wasn't being followed, she took the exit for her friend's house, where Rhonda was waiting for her with an extra large glass of chilled pinot grigio. The friends stayed up a couple of hours talking about tonight's experiences. Finally Toni had calmed down enough, and had consumed sufficient wine, to attempt sleep.

It was a fitful beginning, but finally Toni took one of her emergency valium she kept for just such an occasion, and she drifted off until 5 am.

After breakfast the next morning, Toni drove off to her morning status report. Once she got to the seventh floor conference room, she was surprised to find Captain Bernardo and Doctor Zuniga sitting at the table. It was only 7:55, but the squad and the observers were all in place.

Bernardo explained, "Dr. Zuniga heard about the events of last night, and he asked my permission to address the group, which I gave. But before he begins, I want all of you to know that my review of your police work last night showed me that we have the right people on the job. You did everything by the book, no cowboy heroics," he said looking at Starr, " and no breakdown in police procedure. With that, the floor is yours, Dr. Zuniga."

Zuniga began slowly. "I heard about what had happened last night, then got the full story from the Captain here. I only wanted you to all know that you must be close to something. This man is like a tiger pacing in a cage, trying to look for weaknesses. It is imperative that you be aware of your surroundings, and stay close to those that you trust. He's not finished, in my opinion, and I think that his actions last night are indicative of that fact. So my advice to you is to remain alert and on guard." With that, he rose to leave and said, "And if any of you are feeling depressed, frustrated, whatever, call me. I'll always have time to talk."

He closed the door behind him, when he left. About five seconds later, Billy said, "And we pay him for this bullshit? Of course we're all alert, just look at what happened last night. An eight year old could have told us to be careful, we don't need him to go off about it."

Bernardo tried to defend him, to no avail. Then he got serious, being a cop again, if only for a moment. "Guys, I didn't say this but, don't you see through him? He wants to write a book. And the more times he can be involved, the greater his credibility becomes. In the end, it'll be him that solves the thing...in his book. His coming in here was all for show, all for a book."

The group was impressed by his more than candid observation, especially Toni. "OK," Bernardo asked, "is there anything you're not telling me?"

Everyone looked around the room at the other members of the task force. Toni spoke up. "Not yet." she said, "We might have something in a few days, but nothing yet, that could we could use as hard evidence."

The captain said, "I can live with that. But, only as long as you promise to bring anything solid to me first. I'm getting the pressure as well. And the press don't even know about last night. If they find out, all hell will break loose in this building, and I don't want to be the one person without a chair when the music stops. Are we clear?" "Crystal," Toni replied, "Crystal clear, Captain Bernardo." The captain rose from his seated position, scanning the faces of the group before him. "No matter how phony Zuniga was, be careful. Don't let yourself get caught alone in a dangerous situation. Use and depend on each other," he said as he left.

Toni rose to take charge of the meeting. Everyone knew about last night. Toni reiterated the warnings they had just heard from the doctor and the Captain. Starr broke her silence, and said, "Yeah, last night I was going to be that cowboy. Man, when I think about it now, I realize how lucky I was that it turned out the way it did." Every one murmured their approval, and vowed to stick together.

Toni finished the meeting with, "It's not ideal folks, very little to go on, but I'm a believer that the harder we work, the luckier we get. I want to focus our search in the downtown area. The two possible sightings of this man were both down here, in our backyard. Walk the streets, be aware, and don't go down any dark alleys alone. You're all dismissed." Toni walked over to the non-cop, Adrian. "Are you still OK?" she asked. "After last night, I wouldn't blame you if you wanted off the team." Adrian said, "No, and I held something back from you. I wanted you to see it, outside the group. Another email message." Adrian Keller took a piece of paper out of her purse and showed it to Toni. It read:

Almost!

Next Time You Won't Be So Lucky

The Taker

Toni left and went to Captain Daniels office to fill him in on the short meeting they had with Zuniga and Bernardo present. This was her job. She wasn't going to cut him out of the loop. After she told him of Bernardo's comments about the doctor, Don felt much more comfortable...it had just been a "dog and pony show." Toni also told him of the warning email from "The Taker". Daniels asked, "Are you any closer?" Toni responded cryptically, "Don, there's something there. I don't know what, but I should by the end of the week. That's all I can say right now, with any confidence."

Toni was to meet the locksmith at her home at noon to review the new locks and security equipment she would have installed. Besides the usual deadbolts and steel doors, she would have bolts on the bottom of her doors which could be inserted into the slab. No one could get through that. And, the locksmith would use some of the newest window security items on the 12 casement windows Toni had, along with wireless motion detectors.

A person could still get in, but it would take a while, set off quite a racket with the alarm, and Toni had the Glock. She met him, inspected the layout and design, and approved it. The locksmith said, "This is what I would install for my own daughter. You'll be 100% safe. But like I tell her, look behind you before you open the door entering the house. That's where the danger lies."

About 2:00, Toni was having a late lunch at an outdoor café downtown. It was late February, and the weather was starting to warm up, already. Her cell phone rang, and she saw it was Rosa. Toni answered with "Give me some good news."

Rosa responded with "Marta called, she's found a trail. She says it's a big money trail. Something about laundering illegal drug money. Are you available?" Rosa asked. "I'm halfway there, wherever we're going," Toni said. Rosa gave her the location, "1622 West Sunset, right off Highway 281, it's Marta's house, and office at home. She'll meet us at 4."

"Call Tom, Toni said. "Already did," Rosa said, "he'll meet us there." Toni asked, "I'm inviting the lieutenant, if you don't think Rosa will be intimidated. I'd like him to share in this."

Rosa said, "As long as I vouch for him, she'll be fine. If I tell her it may help her in getting a reward, she'll make him dinner," Rosa laughed.

Toni made the call to the lieutenant. He was excited, just to leave the office, but even more so if there could be a break in the case. She was honest with him. "It may or may not be about The Taker. The lead we stumbled on, better yet, what Rosa led us to, connects the companies where the murder victims were employed. This is the linkage we started looking for in the beginning."

At just before 4 pm the group had converged on a little stucco house, in a very rough neighborhood. It was neat on the outside, the lawn freshly cut, no mildew on the exterior, and the bushes were trimmed. The roof was another matter. It looked like those NSA listening posts you see on TV. It contained at least a dozen antenna, satellite dishes, and other receiving equipment.

Rosa rang the bell and a boy of about six opened the door. Rosa said in her most motherly way, "We're to see your mom, Marta."

Marta suddenly appeared, and said, "Jose, these are

friends of mine. You go to your room later and mama will let you say goodbye when they leave."

Introductions were made all around, and the ball was in Marta's court. She sat in her living room and explained, "I found a pattern which I want to share with you. I think it's only the tip of the iceberg, but I think it's something big. I'm working on it in my office now, she pointed down the hall, and I should be able to follow the trail, and see how widespread it is."

She went on, "As you know, he Mexican drug lords have adopted the organizational structure developed by the cartels in Columbia." The cops looked at each other with amazement. Marta commented, "Don't tell me you didn't know that, everyone knows about that, it's been going on for years. It's a two pronged approach, money laundering, and drug smuggling.

In Columbia, it's Cocaine. Here it mostly involves methamphetamine, grass, and some heroin. It made sense to them. From Dallas, south to the border towns of Mexico like Juarez, Nuevo Laredo, and others, there is a greater population than the country of Columbia. Plus, they save a lot on shipping costs. Anyway, I focused on one obvious site, Brownsville. It sits equidistant between Laredo, Corpus Christi, and Monterrey, which is a collection point.

Daniels interrupted, "A collection point for what?"

"Money," said Marta. "For the drugs sold along the border in Mexico. Large, cash, deposits require an explanation, even in Mexico, so they bring it here. They bring the money, after they take their cut, across the border. Police dogs don't smell money, and they deposit it into a U.S. bank."

Toni questioned this, "Doesn't that cause a 'red flag' on the account? Aren't banks supposed to report all cash deposits over $10,000?" "Right," said Marta, "so they have to find a 'friendly bank', that is one who will split up the cash into deposits of less that $10,000, without reporting it."

The cops looked at each other. Toni spoke for them all, "Don't tell me it's The Alamo Bank and Trust."

Marta looked up, "How'd you know?" Toni said, "It doesn't matter, please continue."

"Well, every week, the bank wires the drug money into an account in the Cayman Islands. This particular Alamo Bank and Trust uses an account named 'Avocado Farmers Union', of which there is no record on file. The money is immediately redirected, with a small commission deducted, to an account in San Antonio's Alamo Bank and Trust, called Tex-Mex Retail Limited, and the money is 100% clean. They can invest it and own restaurants, office buildings, anything," she said.

Marta added, "I've found the identical situation in El Paso. Yes, there's an Alamo Bank and Trust in El Paso which receives and wires the money." They use an account, 'United Lettuce Growers', another 'dummy company' who receives the money in the Caymans, and wires it back here but that's as far as I've gotten."

"What about the drug side of the system?" Tom asked.

Marta answered, "That's a little more conventional. The cash from the drugs sold in El Paso, Corpus Christi, Brownsville, and Laredo, the border towns, probably go into the same pool of cash as the funds from across the border. The drugs sold further north, here, in San Antonio, Austin, and Dallas, they deal with a little more generously. The gangs get a bigger percent, just to keep them happy and gives them operating money, but the wholesalers probably step on the drugs a little harder, that is reduce its' purity, to make it go farther.

Don't forget, up here the control of the gangs is imperative. It keeps others from moving in on the Cartel's territory, so they must keep the gangs happy. In Mexico they have more influence with the police and the courts. Here, they have to use intimidation and muscle, to keep order, and to keep out any competition."

Marta looked up. "By the end of the week I'll have all of it nailed down, definitely the 'shell companies', and probably the names of the people involved."

Lieutenant Daniels asked, "Does this put you in any danger?"

Marta smiled, and said, "Just living here in this neighborhood, puts me in danger, that's why I'm looking for a way out. But, to answer your specific question, no, not as long as you four keep your mouths shut, I'll be OK. I don't think they're sophisticated enough to know I've been in their system, and I leave no trail." She finished with, "I'll call Rosa on Thursday or Friday at the latest."

The cops said goodbye to Jose, and rather than stand on Marta's front lawn drawing unwanted attention, they jumped back into their vehicles and drove away. On the cell phones they all agreed to cancel the usual meeting at 5, and get together in Lt. Daniels office, once they got back to the station. They couldn't get there fast enough...heads were spinning like tops."We've opened a can of worms, now," Daniels said, once the group was back in the SAPD building and they were all standing in front of his desk, with the door closed. "Can all of this drug cartel business be real? And then, how can we link it back to the murders by The Taker?"

Toni spoke up, "My suggestion would be to let Marta get all the information possible, that is the accounts, the key people involved, at least on our side of the border, and see what we've got. We already know that Tex-Mex is funding the mall on I-35, let's sit tight, and work our Taker leads for a couple more days. Marta said she'd have all the facts in by the weekend. "

Tom Granger admonished the group, "We've got to be completely silent on this revelation we received today. No one outside this office can know what that woman is working on. If what she's found is true, there's a great deal of money at stake. If someone finds out, her, and her boy's lives are over, no second thought, no mercy, just gone."

Twenty Five

Wednesday and Thursday went by with their usual meetings, nothing much from the press, and thankfully, no more killings. Adrian Keller had received no more messages, so she wasn't around as much.

Toni, Rosa, and Tom attempted to show interest in walking the streets, showing photos, and questioning possible witnesses It was a façade, of course, and more than once Starr or Billy asked what was on Toni's mind.

"I'm just thinking about moving back home tonight," Toni answered both of them on Wednesday, and they seemed to buy that answer for now. It was easier for Tom. He wasn't in charge of the operation, and he was quiet by nature, so no one was questioning his silence. Rosa stayed busy working any old leads she had from family and friends of the murder victims.

Finally, at 4 pm on Thursday, Rosa got the call. Marta said, "I've got everything. Dates, account numbers, amounts of money transferred, registered owners of the 'shell companies', names of the bankers involved, all of it. It's even bigger than I thought."

Rosa asked, "How long to put into a form which is easily understandable, by cops, I mean."

"A couple of hours, tops," Marta replied. "Great," Rosa said. "And none too soon," Marta added. "Maybe I'm just paranoid, but there have been some gangbangers cruising by my house, my phone has rung with no one on the other end, I'm getting a little shaky."

Rosa thought for a minute and said, "I'll be there in an hour. My girls and I will spend the night with you while you're organizing everything. Then we'll make our case at the police station tomorrow morning. Will that make you feel better?"

Marta tried to argue, but it was a weak attempt. Rosa could tell that yes, it made her feel safer. The four cops met in the Lieutenant's office, within five minutes of Rosa hanging up with Marta.

It was decided that they would make their findings known at 8 am tomorrow morning. Lt. Daniels wanted the Captain to be present, and no one had a problem with that. "Just don't tell him what it's about, yet," Toni asked. "I still don't want to let this out, prematurely." Rosa announced her decision to spend the night at Marta's, all were in agreement there, as well.

Tom Granger was determined, saying, "I'm going to be part of the 'babysitting' detail too. Me and my Smith 357. It can't hurt." Rosa nodded, and Toni wondered if he was afraid for Marta, and her boy, the information, Rosa and her girls, or all of the above. Either way, it was added protection. Tom looked at Rosa and said, "Call and tell her I'll be there in 20 minutes."

Tom kept a change of clothes in his locker, just for an occasion like this. He grabbed his clothes on a hanger, his shaving kit, and was out of SAPD headquarters in 5 minutes. After knocking on the door to make sure everything was OK, Tom pulled Dodge Ram around the side of Marta's house, away from prying eyes. About 45 minutes later, Rosa and her girls showed up, and to Tom's happy surprise they were both wearing the hats he had bought them this past weekend. Maria and Anna took over entertaining Jose, while Tom and Rosa did a preliminary check of all the doors and windows. The doors had strong locks and the windows were all barred, even the ones in the doors. "Looks copasetic to me," Tom declared.

"I feel so safe, so important," Marta declared. Rosa kidded her, "We just want the paperwork, we'd give you up in a minute," and she laughed. "And we've known each other for how many years?" Rosa said. "Even the nuns thought we were sisters."

"Yes, but I was always the younger one," Marta shot back. "You've got me there," Rosa admitted.

Tom asked, "I brought a bottle of wine and some Corona at lunchtime today. OK if I put them in your refrigerator? Everything else will be fine outside." Marta smiled, "Fine, as long as you don't expect to find them all there in the morning."

"I was kinda hoping you'd say that," Tom grinned back.

Marta looked at Jose and said, "Mama's going back to work in her office, you stay here with the girls. Show them your toys, and share." Rosa looked at Maria, "Don't answer the door for anyone, postman, fireman, no one, understood?" Maria knew when her mom meant business, and this was one of those times.

The two adults walked back to Marta's office. They hadn't seen much on the visit earlier this week, but there was a network of 4 computers, fiber optic and cable internet connections, and networking supporting six monitors. "Looks like NASA in here," Tom said. "Hardly," Marta said. "Each of these computers has 1000 times the power of what we took to the moon in '69."

As if to emphasize her point, Marta elaborated. "Tom, your cell phone has more capacity than those first astronauts had available to them. The more I know about computer history, that moon landing was made with stone age technology, hard working engineers, a load of luck, and excuse me, a lot of balls. Hell, Rosa, they were still using slide rules at mission control."

Marta finished her lecture with "The Apollo 11 went to the moon and back with a computer memory of 2K, and a speed of 1-MHZ. Technology-wise to today, that's more of a difference than the Wright brother's plane to an F-15."

"OK," Marta switched gears, "let's talk about the thing which brought you here, and is hopefully going to get me and Jose out of this jungle."

"I've identified five accounts which send money to the Cayman Accounts, and is then redirected back to San Antonio. All the money originates at the Alamo Bank and Trust Branches:

1) El Paso... "Union Lettuce Growers"
2) Del Rio... "Associated Maize Importers"
3) Laredo... "Felipe's Leather Goods"
4) Brownsville... "Avocado Farmer's Union"
5) Houston... "United Fruit & Vegetable"

All of these are, of course, bogus, shell companies.

"Then," Marta continued, "there are three more branch banks, one each in Austin, Dallas, and San Antonio, which all deposit into the main account, using the name Texas Development Committee, which then gets deposited into Tex-Mex Retail, just like the wired accounts from the Caymans. The next page illustrates the money trail."

Cash Trail

Money to Caymans...Money to San Antonio

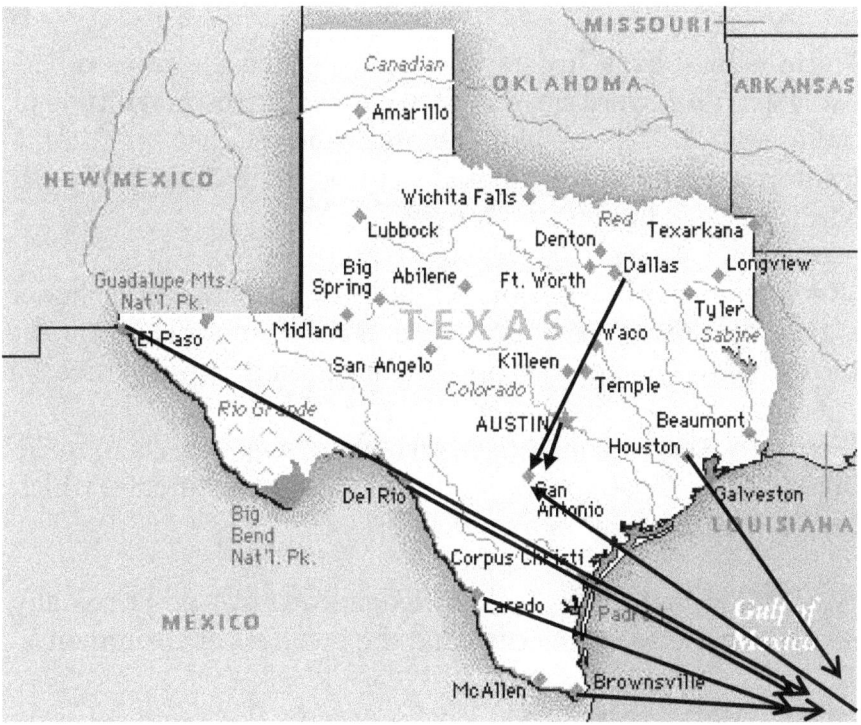

To Caymans then on to San Antonio: (1) El Paso, (2) Del Rio, (3) Laredo, (4) Brownsville, (5) Houston...All from Alamo Bank and Trust Branches.

Directly from Alamo Bank and Trust to main Bank in San Antonio: (1) Dallas, (2) Austin, and (3) San Antonio local cash.

Rosa, and Tom were stunned by the enormity of the operation. Toni asked, "How long has this been going on." Rosa replied, "As far as I can tell it began in El Paso, about six years ago. All the accounts there on the map have been operational for at least three years."

Tom asked, "I've got the $64,000 question," he said. How much money are we talking about?"

Marta leaned back in her chair and studied the faces of the two cops. They were clearly overwhelmed by the magnitude of the operation. Marta said, "Before I answer that question, I want you to know that there is a lot more than just cash holdings we're talking about here."

"Remember that the reason behind this Cartel business model is two-fold. First, they need to clean the money. That way, at the end of the process, no one can question the cash source."

"Secondly, the reason to have a viable cash source, is to make investments. Good, solid, money making investments, which they can operate out in the open."

"We follow that," Rosa acknowledged, we just don't see any connection between the cash and the business environment."

"Well," Marta responded, "that's exactly the point." If you hadn't been investigating these murders, and the executives at some of the companies hadn't lied to my friend, Rosa, why would you have dug deeper into the affiliation of several seemingly outstanding companies?"

"These are Chamber of Commerce / San Antonio, type organizations, all with impeccable records, including those of their employees, which I gather from Rosa. They had to hire the cleanest people, to avoid any undue attention. Now look at this list."

Tex-Mex Holdings

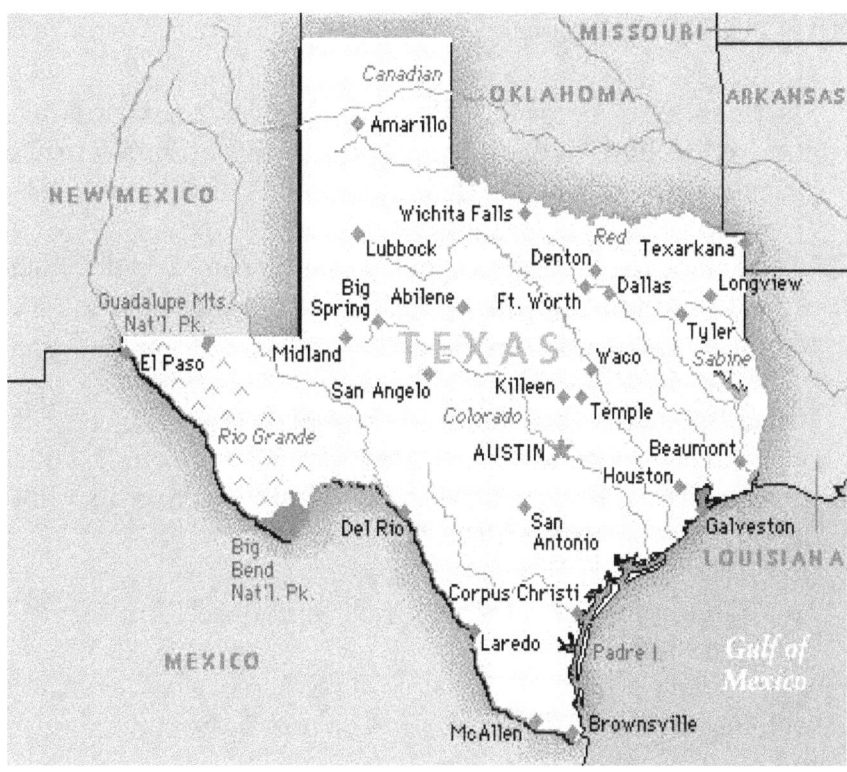

- Tex-Mex Real Estate...11 Apartment Complexes

- Tex-Mex Resort...5 Hotels, 2 Golf Courses

- Tex-Mex Transportation...2 Truck Lines

- Tex-Mex Food...8 restaurants, 1 food importer

- Tex-Mex Retail...5 shopping centers, 1 under construction

Marta finally said, as all the cops gaped at the chart, "Tom, to answer your question, these five accounts, and there may be more, have on deposit with Alamo Bank and Trust, just the main bank, over one hundred eighteen million dollars. That's as of 5 pm yesterday."

Marta added, "As far as I can tell, they have run over five hundred million dollars through those five accounts in the past six years, paying for their apartments, hotels, etc."

"And you have records for all of this?" Tom asked. Marta replied, "Account numbers, deposit dates, wire transaction numbers, I've got it all covered."

Marta finished, "One hundred sixty eight pages of records, right off the web. Is this a great country or what? I just didn't want to bore you with the detail, when a map and little arrows are much more to the point."

Tom interrupted, "And what juries want to see. But this will never go to trial."

"Why not?" asked Rosa. "Yeah, why not?" Marta demanded to know.

"Oh, they'll go to jail. They'll go away for a long time. You think the lawyers are stupid enough to put this up in front of a jury. Any juror you'd seat, has lost someone to the gangs. Maybe a sister OD'd, maybe a cousin was forced to join, and got himself killed at eleven years old, or a baby was killed in a 'drive-by' shooting."

"All that anguish, so these fools could line their pockets with 'blood money', no siree, they'll want to settle." And there, Marta, is your ticket out of this place. Once the State

Boys are done with them, the IRS will be up their ass with a microscope. You'll get ten percent of whatever they collect, and it looks like this was a cash business with plenty to collect from." Tom looked at the others an said, "Don't know about you girls, but I'm getting myself a beer, and buying the first round."

The group gladly accepted the invitation, and they went into the kitchen and sat around the table. Marta commented, "I wasn't very good at planning this, but I've got enough cabrito in the freezer to feed an army. Sound OK to you?" There was no argument there.

After dinner, Tom called Toni at home, and filled her in on the discoveries so she wouldn't be caught off guard, tomorrow morning. She, in turn called the lieutenant, so he would be aware of what information they were bringing in to the captain.

Twenty Six

The next morning a small convoy descended on the SAPD headquarters at 7:30. Tom drove Marta, and had all the records and maps behind the seat.

Rosa followed with the three children. Today, and maybe for a few days, they'd be staying out of class. Rosa had called her girls' principal, so had Marta.

They went up to seven, making a quick stop at Lt. Daniels office, to pick him up for the meeting, and deposit the kids in his office. Strict instructions were given. "Stay in your seat, and touch nothing. Anyone comes in here, don't say a word." Rosa pulled the venetian blinds and Daniels locked the door behind him. They took the elevator up, and Captain Bernardo was already on his second cup of coffee, waiting for them.

Two hours later, they were all exhausted. The primary objective was met, however. Although they hadn't yet connected this to murder victims, Bernardo saw, laid out before him, the largest criminal undertaking of his career.

"We're going to need help with this," he said. We can't prosecute with tainted evidence, but this will point the State Investigators (still called the Texas Rangers) to the right places. Getting warrants should be no problem. Company D, headquarters is two buildings away. They have jurisdiction for the entire state. I'll have their commander, who I went to school with, and some of their best criminal and internet investigators here in an hour. You feel up to going through everything with them?" Marta nodded, and the meeting was set.

For the next week, Toni was able to concentrate on The Taker case again. None of those that knew, commented on the conspiracy investigation, to anyone. However, they were just going through the motions at this point, waiting for all hell to break loose on the "Tex-Mex" front, and hoping to catch a break in the murder case. There had been no new murders in the past week. Toni wasn't sure if that was good news or bad.

Starr, Billy, all of the task force were still pressing to find the killer. If they didn't find him soon, they would probably be finding another victim.

Toni and Tom had developed a theory. Off the wall, but better than nothing. Someone was mad at Tex-Mex. A former partner in one of the businesses involved, a disgruntled employee, whatever. But someone was getting the authorities to look more closely into the complicit companies. The question was, who?

The next morning was ten days after the money laundering scam was revealed to the state authorities. The news media were all over the case laid out by the state and local authorities. Some of the bylines included:

Local Bank Assets Seized

Drug Money Behind New Mall

Over $150 Million Frozen in Accounts

Former Governor May Be Involved

FDIC and IRS Join Investigation

Gang Money Cut Off at Source

This was the beginning of the end for Tex-Mex, the companies involved in the operation, and would take a big chunk out of the gangs overall capabilities.

A big positive in the bust was that Marta and her son had won the lottery, so to speak. She was in line for a big payday from the IRS, and State of Texas, in their crime fighting campaign. It might take six months to collect, but, as Tom had predicted, the partners were dealing, admitting guilt for favorable treatment at sentencing time.

Once the authorities had two or three who would testify, there would be no more deals, so the people involved were tripping over each other to become "States Evidence."

As for the gangs, without money or drugs for even just a few days, they would start to turn on each other, leaving the local populace alone, for a while. It was time for the task force to refocus on the murders, but the trail was getting colder.

The cops had searched the streets, bars, hangouts, pool halls, you name it. Billy had even gone to all the men's clothing stores which specialized in outfitting Big and Tall men. The shopkeepers had many customers who fit the general description of the man they suspected to be "The Taker", but none stood out from the rest.

At the next task force meeting, everyone was still buzzing about the busts, and lamenting the lack of progress in their own case. It was frustrating.

Adrian Keller came into the room with more news. It was another email from "The Taker." "This came in just this morning," she said. "I don't think there's any question of who sent it, It's the same guy as before."

She handed the paper to Toni, who read it to the group. It said:

You Have Effectively Dealt With The Gangs

And Those Who Supported Them

My Mission is Over

I Am Disappeared With The Wind

The Taker

Toni studied the email for a moment. Her face turning red with anger. "This monster kills five people, and now expects us to turn away?" Toni called Lieutenant Daniels, and asked him to join the discussion. He came up in five minutes, bringing Captain Bernardo with him.

She read the message to them, and waited for their reaction. Bernardo said exactly what Toni was thinking.

"Murderers don't get to kill innocent people, and then have the option to call a 'time out' because their vendetta is over," Bernardo said. "I want this monster caught," he said, and left the room.

"I'm even more intent on getting this guy, if that's possible," Toni said. "But don't forget, be careful. He knows where we live."

This was the consensus among all those in the room. The email had exactly the opposite effect which had been intended by the sender. It served to inflame, even to galvanize those who had worked so hard to apprehend the killer. "We're on this case," Toni said, "and we'll stay on it to the end." She added, "Tom, I guess you might want to tell the group about our little theory. Sounds like we were close."

Tom stood and began, "We thought that whoever was killing these people, Ruiz, the gang leader excluded, had it out for Tex-Mex, and was trying to lead us to uncover their money laundering scheme."

"Now, it looks like there is an ulterior, companion motive. Yeah, this Taker guy was leading us to connect the dots between the companies, but his motive was still, to put the clamps on the gangs, which we just did."

The more the group discussed the possibility, the more they liked the idea. Even Lt. Daniels agreed that it was a solid factor in the investigation.

"Adrian," Toni asked, "how's the list of gang killers who were exonerated coming? Let's revisit that."

"I can have a complete work-up, by date, for the 5 pm meeting today," Adrian said, and left the room.

Toni pulled Billy aside and said, "It's time for the planted story, make the call." He knew exactly what she was talking about, they'd discussed it with the lieutenant. She turned back to the group, "We'll meet back here at 5, and start working the list in teams of two, this guy knows who we are. She looked at Daniels and asked, can you give us a hand for a couple of days?" He answered, "Of course "I'll work with Rosa, she's been interviewing the corporations by herself, but now, no one should be alone."

At 5 pm, Toni divided up the list between the three groups. She had asked Adrian to print the list alphabetically, and gave each group about one third of the interviews. It was a big list, numbering about 150 names for each set of investigators.

At 6 pm, the planted story made the news...big time.

"This is Rita Estrada, Channel 13 News. We have just now heard from a reliable police source close to The Taker investigation that the task force has narrowed it's search to that of one individual. This SAPD source confirms that an arrest is imminent, possibly within the next 48 hours. We'll give you more as the facts come in."

Despite the announcement, the next morning, the group all began their tasks. Members of the ask Force were asking Toni about the news on TV, and she just shrugged her head, "Don't know, and couldn't talk about it if I did."

Some of their search required good detective work, just to find the people on the list. Many had moved out of town, some were in extended family situations, and others just wouldn't talk to the police, no matter what. Then there were people who had died, divorced, or who were now in retirement homes.

Toni asked the group of investigators gathered at the 5 pm meeting, plus Adrian Keller, from I.T., "What are we missing people?" Billy answered, "Maybe we haven't gone back far enough." The groans around the room told Toni that this wasn't the problem.

Rosa asked, "I know we're looking at murders in the past 5 years, where 'justice' was supposedly not served. But what about house fires, car wrecks, 1st degree assaults, and other violent acts?"

Toni thought for a moment, and then asked Adrian, "Can we look into those things as well?" Adrian shrugged her shoulders, "Sure, but that will be an even larger list."

"OK," Toni decided, "Adrian, start on that list, violent crimes in the past five years where the perp walked, witnesses recanted, or which were pled down. If we don't get results from the murder list, we'll start on the new list, next week, if we still need it," she said cryptically.

Toni finished with, "Alright people, let's get home, and get some rest. Tomorrow's going to be another day just like this one, but we may get lucky. No morning meeting, hit the streets early."

The next day came and went without any solid results or leads. Another large dose of frustration for the task force. "It looks like we're more than half way through this group," Toni said. "We may be going to 'plan B' sooner than I thought."

She asked, "How's the list coming, Adrian?" The I.T. person seemed a little defensive and said, "It's going to be a much bigger list than this one you're working now, but it's in the works."

Toni responded, "I know we're all a little frustrated. Today's Friday, I don't think we have any more bodies coming in, at least that's what the email said, so let's recharge and come in on Monday with a fresh approach."

The meeting broke up, and people scattered. Tom was going over to Rosa's tonight, supposedly to visit her girls, Billy was going to be with Rita, Starr had a date. And Toni was alone. Rhonda was on a buying trip. So she took her time leaving the office. About halfway home, her cell phone rang, the number was familiar, but she couldn't place it.

She answered "Ramos here." There was a quiet voice on the other end. It was Adrian Keller, from I.T., and she was whispering.

"This is probably silly," Adrian said softly, "but I stopped off to get some groceries, and I saw a very large man looking at me, you know like the one in the description. So I got in my car and drove about four blocks to the butcher I use. I parked and got out, but he was closed, I just missed him. He usually is open till 6, but since it's Friday, he probably left early."

Adrian was still whispering, "So then I start to go back to my car, and there he was again. The big man was walking straight toward my car. So I turned around and went into the first open store I saw. It was a club, but I went in anyway, and sat on a stool at the bar." Toni was thinking, Billy's "planted story" flushed him out, but why pick Adrian? "So where is he now?" Toni asked.

"He came in, looked around and took a booth in the corner. He's still here." Toni asked, "Exactly where are you? I'm on the way." Adrian said, "I'm probably over reacting, aren't I? he's made no move to hurt me."

Toni repeated, "Exactly where are you?"

Adrian whispered, "A little place called 'Cervesa y Mas' on Houston and Walters, downtown."

"Whatever you do, don't leave, even if he does. I'll be there in ten." Toni pulled off of Highway 281 at the next exit, made two lefts and re-entered the same Highway going southbound. She pulled off the Houston Street east, exit and rolled to a stop across the street from the bar. She entered and slowly scanned the area. Her eyes finally adjusted to the darkness. There was Adrian, sitting on a stool, sipping a beer, trying to look natural. Toni sat down next to her. She could see the big, Hispanic, man in the mirror hung over the bar. He was huge alright, with a straw western hat, and overalls.

Adrian said, "Thanks for coming. I'm pretty sure he would have tried something by now if he was out to get me, but he hasn't. He's just sitting over there by himself. I guess there's no crime in that."

"No," Toni said, "but you can't be too careful, and I had a slow night planned, anyway. You know, better safe than sorry."

"What, no hot date?" Adrian asked. "No, Toni grinned, my job pretty much is my life, but I guess you've seen that."

"Well, I hope I didn't embarrass myself too much, can we keep it to ourselves, or did you call in the cavalry?" Adrian asked. "No, just me," Toni answered. Adrian said, "Let me buy you a beer for your trouble."

"No, that's not necessary," Toni replied. Toni saw the disappointment in Adrian's face and rescued her denial with, "But a glass of Pino Grigio would be great."

Adrian beamed and flagged down the bartender to order the wine. Just then, the big man got up from his booth, and without so much as a glance toward the two women, left the bar.

The wine was served, and they had a small toast, "to being careful." Toni said, Drink slowly. Let's wait about ten minutes before we leave, give him a chance to go away.

"Speaking of going," Toni said, "Would you excuse me for a moment? I had way too much coffee this afternoon, and now the wine, I'll be right back."

"Sure," said Adrian, "when you gotta go, you gotta go. Nothing wrong with that."

Toni asked, and the bartender pointed out a little sign which said "Los Banos", with an arrow pointing right around the corner.

Toni left her stool and headed around the corner. Once she was in the ladies room she took out her cell phone, trying to decide to use it or not. What had she just told Adrian? Better safe, than...she knew procedure.

She dialed Tom Granger's number, he picked it up on the second ring. "Granger", he answered.

"Tom I've got a strange situation here. A large Hispanic man followed Adrian Keller after work. We flushed him out with the phony news story. She saw him at three different places. She went into a bar, and he followed her. inside."

Tom asked, "Did you call for backup?" Toni shook her head, "No, Tom, in fact he's gone now, but he could be waiting outside. It's dark now, but Adrian doesn't want to make a big deal out of it, and thinks she's being foolish. I want to play this out a little longer, to be sure."

"I'll be right there, Tom said. "No, that's not necessary," said Toni as she rethought the situation, "but I'll leave my cell phone on, in my pocket, and give you an update without Adrian knowing it. Once we get out of here, I'll give you the all clear." Tom said, "You're the boss, but scream to high heaven if something goes down. You're only three minutes to the station. Plenty of cops there."

Toni slipped the cell phone in her jacket pocket, and returned to the bar. Adrian was still smiling, all seemed right with the world.

"I've got to go home, said Adrian, let's finish our drinks, I'm sure he's long gone by now. I'll go to the ladies room, and we'll go when I come back."

Toni took a long swallow, of the wine...not bad. Then she finished it off. By the time Adrian returned, she was feeling a little giddy. "You OK?" asked Adrian. "On one glass of wine?" Toni laughed, "Of course. The cool air will help as well." They walked to the door, stepped down the exit, and the lights went out.

Twenty Seven

Tom heard the chatter stop, and then, Adrian's voice say "Put her in the trunk, like the others." He was signaling Rosa, while he kept his ear to the phone, he didn't want to be overheard on the open cell phone.

About ten seconds later he listened to the sound of a car trunk being slammed shut. Tom finally was able to talk, "Rosa, they've got Toni."

"Who?" she asked. "I believe it's The Taker, and Adrian is in on it. I've got to use your phone to call for help. Rosa had Lt. Daniels on speed dial, Tom switched phones with her, "Listen for any hints to where they're taking her. She's in the trunk of a car, somewhere downtown."

Daniels finally answered his phone. Tom hurriedly, but effectively detailed the situation. As luck would have it, the lieutenant was still at SAPD when Tom's call came in. He connected to the dispatcher who put out the APB, "Officer Down, repeat, Officer Down. Last seen less than five minutes ago leaving 'Cervesa y Mas', corner of Houston and Walters. Officer believed to be held in trunk of suspects' car. Suspects described as Hispanic male, 6'5", 275 pounds, and white female, 5'4", 120 pounds. Consider both armed and dangerous. All officers please respond."

While the call was going out, Daniels was calling his counterpart with the Texas State Troopers. They would have checkpoint roadblocks to the entrances at I-10, I-35, and Highway 281. Additionally the police would stop and search all vehicles with trunks on Commerce and Houston Streets.

Tom hung up with the lieutenant and looked at Rosa, "I'm going downtown," as they swapped cell phones, again. "Not without me," she declared, "I'm going too."

"I don't have time to argue," he said. "You remember the last time we were baited into going downtown. He circled back behind us, and kicked in Toni's door. You can't leave your girls."

"I'm not arguing, we'll drop them at my cousin Sylvia's house. It's on the way. No one would think they would be there." Rosa grabbed her Beretta PX 4, 9mm, and yelled, "Girls, get in the truck."

Daniels had called Captain Bernardo who (after the fact) OK'd everything which Tom had set in motion. "Didn't have time to ask permission," he said. "You did fine," the captain assured him. "Meet me on four," Daniels yelled to the captain, "I've got an idea."

Pete Moore, the head of I.T. was there. Daniels asked, "Can you track an open cell phone?" The man said, "Sure, if you've got the number." Daniels wrote it down and said, "Get on it, Officer Down!" With that statement and the captain standing right behind him, Moore sprung into action. He gathered all three of his staff and they began a triangulation cell tower search, immediately, starting with downtown.

"I'm short one person, tonight, but we should be able to get a fix on the signal in five minutes or so. Adrian Montoya, went home early, when she was finished with your work," Moore said. "You mean Adrian Keller?" Daniels asked. "Yeah," said Pete Moore, "I keep calling her by her married name. She's always correcting me, but her 'ex' is a hard man to forget." Daniels asked, "What do you mean by that?" Moore looked up from his computer screen. "You don't know, do you?" Captain Bernardo interrupted, "Why don't you explain what you're talking about, while you work, please."

Moore said, "The system is searching block by block, I just have to move the center, occasionally, so I'm good."

"Have either of you heard of Manny Montoya?" Bernardo said, "Yes, I met him years ago, at a local celebrity function. He went by Manny 'The Mountain' Montoya. Huge guy, I met him, once in Austin, so what."

"That's Adrian's ex-husband. He was ranked in the top three in the world, a real contender in MMA, Mixed Martial Arts, for you lieutenant. Of course, all that was before the incident."

"What incident?" asked Daniels. "Wow," Moore said. "Manny came home early one day. He was supposed to be in Houston, but a match got cancelled two days before. His opponent was injured while training, and no one else would take the fight on such short notice."

"Anyway, he and Adrian had a 9-year old daughter. Manny walked into his home and heard her screaming. Two gang members were taking their turns with her, if you know what I mean. Manny surprised them, even though they had a lookout on the street honking his horn when he saw Manny walk in, they didn't hear the warning over the screams." Bernardo and Daniels gave each other a stunned look, this was the link.

"Anyway," Moore continued, "Manny killed one of them with his bare hands. The guy shot him with his 38, but

Manny tore his arm out of the socket, and then broke his neck. The other guy wasn't a match for Manny either. Manny hit him flush on the nose and drove the nasal cartilage right into his brain, instant death."

"Then he ran outside where the car horn was honking, kicked the guy's window in, and dragged him out of the window. Guy had a knife, Manny didn't care. He broke both the guy's legs. Lucky for him, two cruisers pulled up by this time. Two cops had to Taser Manny to put him down."

"Sad part is, the jury let the third guy off with a year inside. He testified that yes, they had someone they were ordered to intimidate, but it was the house across the street. They had made a mistake with the address. He said, he knew nothing about any rape, it wasn't planned. They were just supposed to scare a guy. A guy who lived across the street."

"I remember something about that," Bernardo said. It happened before I came here from the capital. What happened after that?" Bernardo asked.

"The girl is catatonic. Sits and stares out a window all day. She's in a facility in Kerrville. Her name is Emily."

"Manny escaped as well. He crawled into a liquor bottle, never fought again. Of course he was never brought up on charges for defending his daughter, but he never forgave himself."

"And Adrian, well you know about her."

"Not until tonight, we didn't," Bernardo said. "Get a fix on that cell phone. An officer's life is at stake. Do it."

Tom had called Billy Cheatham and Starr from Rosa's cell phone, while he was on his way to drop off her daughters and get downtown. Luckily, both were in the general area. Starr was on the move at once. Billy said, "Rita's with me, what should I do?" Tom screamed, "If it was you in the trunk, what would you like me to do?"

That answered, Billy joined the search, Rita included. Just then dispatch called out, "Be advised, suspects are Manuel Montoya, and Adrian Montoya Keller. Descriptions the same as transmitted before." Tom and Rosa shared a look, both shaking their heads.

Lieutenant Daniels called next, and gave the searchers the background they had uncovered on the Montoya event. Tom remembered what he had observed at two of the crime scenes, "a really strong man."

Twenty Eight

Toni started coming out of the fog which enveloped her brain. She first recognized the musty odor she had encountered at a couple of the crime scenes. She was bound at the feet and hands behind her back. The floor was hard packed dirt. She wasn't blindfolded, and her mouth wasn't taped. She felt the plastic flex-cuffs on her wrists. She used to be limber enough to pull her hands under her legs so that her arms would then be in front of her. Could she still do it? Would it matter?

As her vision started to clear up, she could see that she was on the floor of an old basement. She pretended to stay unconscious. She could hear Adrian arguing with someone on the other side of the room. She whispered, "Tom, if you can hear me, don't say anything. I'm in a basement. I hear Adrian Keller's voice here also. There are some stone steps coming down from the street. I can see a little light, but not much, more later."

She was hoping there would be a later. She could still hear Adrian arguing with a man. Was it the man from the bar, she wondered?

Tom heard the whispered message. He immediately called dispatch. "Tell them I'm in contact with the captive officer. She's in a basement with stone steps coming down from outside. She thinks it's on a street."

He looked at Rosa, "The roadblocks haven't found her. I'm betting she's still in the area." Tom heard the dispatcher get out the message. As he arrived downtown he began cruising the streets around the abduction point, Canton, Belmont, Gibbs, Crockett.

Toni could hear better now. Either they were louder, or she was more awake. She continued to pretend to be unconscious. She was still trying to get her hands in front of her, but she had to proceed very slowly. They were arguing about what to do with her. From what she could make out, the big man didn't want to kill her. Adrian was goading him, "What about Emily? You want her to have no one?" she asked. "Do your part of the job."

Toni saw the big man put his hands on the sides of his head, rubbing it so hard she thought it would split open. He was confused, but he finally nodded to Adrian. "But this is it," he said, rising from a stool. "No more innocent ones will die." Adrian assented, "We have a deal, this is the last one." Manny picked up the large limb cutters hanging on the wall, and started toward Toni.

Rosa's phone rang. Obviously, Billy had the same idea. About cruising around the bar. "I've got a possible sighting on Dakota Street," he barked into the phone. Tom answered, "You driving the Audi?"

"No, Rita's 'Beamer', a red convertible," Billy answered. Tom called the lieutenant's direct line at headquarters for backup. Daniels answered the phone and took down the address.

Toni whispered, "They've decided to kill me, he's coming over." Tom yelled over Rosa's phone, "Billy, go in hard, they're about to finish her off, I'm two blocks away."

Billy leapt out of the car, holding his Colt in front of him, and ran to the door...locked! He kicked it in and saw Manny standing in the middle of the room, with the pair of limb pruners in his hand. Manny moved so quickly he was on Billy in an instant. Billy's rodeo days were behind him, but he thought he could put up a good fight, until Tom got there. He was wrong!

Manny threw him against the stone wall like a rag doll, and Billy was out before he hit the ground. Manny started after him to finish him off, but was startled by a scream from Rita Estrada, standing inside the doorway.

The big man turned toward the door to see Rita get hit from behind by Adrian with a stool. Rita was out.

Tom Granger ran down the steps and into the room. He shoved Adrian to the ground, pointing his 357 magnum at Manny, then at Adrian. "You're both under arrest. Don't move." Manny rushed him, but he had much more distance to cover than when he jumped Billy. Tom fired the revolver twice, hitting the big man in the middle of the chest. Amazingly, he went down to one knee, got up and started toward Tom again. Tom fired two more times, and Manny was gone.

Rosa was right behind Tom. She was keeping Adrian covered until backup arrived. Tom walked over to Toni, she was unhurt, except for the effort it took to finally get her hands in front of her. She was proud of herself for that.

"Backup's here," Rosa announced, as strobe lights hit the small street. With the distraction, Adrian pulled a small revolver out of her jacket pocket, and fired at Tom, striking him in the left shoulder. As Tom went down, Adrian knocked the gun out of Rosa's hand. She said, "You didn't think that big, alcoholic, was The Taker, did you? I orchestrated everything. I found out where the gangs were hiding their blood money and led you right to it. It just took you a little longer to get the answer, because I had to be careful. That big lug, he was just the muscle." She looked around the room, trying to see where the next threat might come from. She walked over to Tom. "I guess you're next, long timer," she said leveling the small pistol at the back of Tom's head.

"Boom" went the report from Toni's Glock. She hit Adrian Keller right in the middle of the forehead, almost blowing the top of the woman's head off. Adrian hadn't noticed Toni's getting her hands in front of her. Then it was just a matter of getting to the weapon in her belt holster, and squeezing off a shot as she had been trained to do, but had never had to, before tonight.

Backup was coming in, prepared for the worst. Shotguns and semi-automatics had safeties off. All the cops held out their badges and raised their hands, until everything was sorted out. Starr came in the basement with the cops, and identified the "good guys." Then, crime scene and medical took over.

As it turned out, both killers were dead, Billy hurt all over his body, Rita had a headache, and Tom said he was only "winged." No one in the small basement would have their full hearing back right away, from all the close range gunfire, but no one was complaining, just talking more loudly.

Rosa, other than being a little embarrassed, was fine. The medics took Billy into the hospital for observation, Tom had to get his wound cleaned and bandaged. Rosa went with him. There might just be something there, in the future, Toni thought.

A Fitting End

The late evening news, was on site. Three, two, one, you're on! "Good evening citizens of San Antonio, this is Rita Estrada, reporting live. As predicted, yesterday by this reporter, the serial killer who called himself The Taker was found, shot and killed this evening along with his accomplice. This daring police action came as a result of undercover work by some of San Antonio's finest, including Detective Toni Ramos, head of the task force hunting this mass killer."

"This reporter was on the actual scene when the action occurred. Police fired only in self defense when attacked. Two of these heroes are now in the hospital, as we speak. Full recovery, is the prognosis for both."

"We'll have more for you at 6 am, but all citizens of the city can sleep a little better, tonight, now that this monster is off the streets."

"Rita Estrada, Channel 13, KBOY News, always first on the scene."

Toni and Lieutenant Daniels were watching from twenty feet away during the report. Daniels said, "She made us sound pretty good, didn't she?"

Toni laughed. "We did promise her an exclusive, after all."

www.ingramcontent.com/pod-product-compliance
Lightning Source LLC
Chambersburg PA
CBHW070303040726
47505CB00020B/1831